FORGOTTEN LANCASHIRE

and Parts of Cheshire and the Wirral

by

Dr Derek J Ripley

FIRST EDITION

TMB BOOKS

First published in Great Britain in 2012
TMB Books is the publishing arm of The Tripe Marketing Board
A division of LEB Ltd
57 Orrell Lane
Liverpool L9 8BX

10% of the profits from the sales of this book will be donated to charities in north west England.

ISBN 978 0 9573141 0 8

British Library Cataloguing in Publication Data.
A catalogue record for this book is available from the British Library.

www.tripemarketingboard.co.uk
www.forgottenlancashire.co.uk
Produced by Stephen Lewis,
Paul Etherington and Nick Broadhead;
Cover Design by Stephen Lewis and Paul Etherington
Interior Design and Layout by Paul Etherington

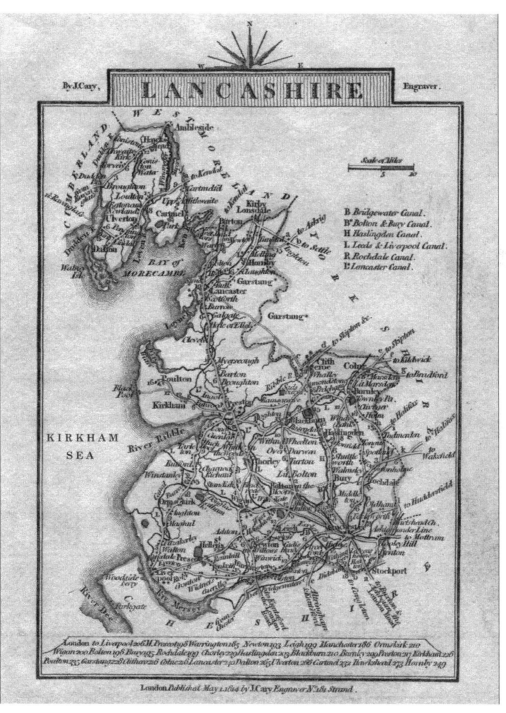

*J Cary's 'Double Garstang' Map of Lancashire printed in 1814,
notable for the fact that Garstang appears in the wrong place twice*

Dedicated to Nataya Ripley

'It is a truth universally acknowledged that
fiction is often considerably
stranger than fact.'

Ethel Austen (1778 — 1865)

It isn't often that I disagree with an eminent businessman, but when Henry Ford said "history is bunk" he was talking rubbish. Here at the Tripe Marketing Board we know that more than most: we are proud to have been a part of history (even if a declining one) for many years.

When Eric Ripley asked us to publish this book about the Lancashire we seem to have forgotten (not to mention parts of Cheshire and the Wirral) I could think of no other person who could present the facts in quite the same way. His reputation as a fine local historian and an even better librarian goes before him.

He has brought to the public a quite astounding collection of documents which recently came to light and which forces us to reappraise our understanding of Lancashire and its people.

After many years languishing on the butchers' slabs of the north west, tripe may also be destined for a reappraisal and might even be about to make a comeback. If it does, it will be in no small part due to the efforts of folk like Eric, who understand the part it has played in the weft and weave of local communities.

I can only commend Mr Ripley's achievement in marshalling such an incredible array of historical facts and figures. I sincerely hope you will enjoy this book as much as we enjoy promoting tripe.

Sir Norman Wrassle
Chairman, The Tripe Marketing Board
Preston

THE JABEZ COWELL LOOKY-LIKEY AGENCY
(NEW BRIGHTON)

FOR THE CONVENIENCE OF THOSE WHO MAY BE INTERESTED J.C.A (NEW BRIGHTON) LTD. WISH TO SUBMIT THE FOLLOWING INFORMATION ABOUT OUR EXTENSIVE PORTFOLIO OF LOOKY-LIKEYS:

GEORGE SPRAGUE (ALFRED TENNYSON, THE POET LAUREATE)

The above looky-likey, born and educated in Rock Ferry, has returned, and is now in Birkenhead permanently. He is available for the opening of commercial premises, hospitals and church fetes. N.B.Though all Mr. Sprague's recent work has been in London, his speech is completely Scouse. Will shave beard for an extra 2s.

AMELIA CORONET (MRS CHRISTINA ROSSETTI, MRS ROSSETTI's TWIN SISTER, MRS ROSSETTI's COUSIN)

Miss Coronet is available for cookery demonstrations at all times and for the presentation of awards to students of domestic science. Will recite Mrs Rossetti's poetry for an additional sum (but has a slight speech impairment). Not willing to display ankles.

ALBERT HARRIS (HG WELLS)

Mr Harris will walk and talk in a perfect facsimile of the famous Mr HG Wells, the writer and time-traveller. Mr Harris' twin brother Franklyn can be available for a small additional fee (currently two guineas) and they can perform an amusing 'time travel' routine. Available for supermarket openings, church bazaars and bar mitzvahs.

HAROLD SWITHINS (BENJAMIN DISRAELI)

Mr Swithins has been our most successful Disraeli Looky-Likey for some 15 years, and can be relied upon to put on a good show. Has a repertoire of card tricks which he can perform when events are running late. Not willing to work in Wales. No reasonable job refused.

THE JABEZ COWELL LOOKY-LIKEY AGENCY
(NEW BRIGHTON)

Mr Cowell would at all times like to assure clients that his agency will use its best endeavours to provide a looky-likey for your occasion. In the unfortunate event that your chosen looky-likey is not available due to indisposition, we reserve the right to substitute with a looky-likey of similar value.

ASK ABOUT OUR DISRAELI / QUEEN VICTORIA DOUBLE BOOKING DISCOUNT.

Are YOU an approximation of someone famous? Then please call at our offices at the Ham & Egg Parade in New Brighton to discuss terms and we will be pleased to represent you.

The Jabez Cowell Looky-Likey Agency in New Brighton was one of over 200 Look-Alike Agencies operating across Lancashire and the Wirral in the late 19th century

CONTENTS

ACKNOWLEDGEMENTS

So many people have contributed to this book that it is impossible to thank them all. An especial debt is owed to the many local history curators and librarians who have ably given of their time and expertise in its preparation. I am particularly grateful to my research assistants Stephen Lewis, Paul Etherington and Nick Broadhead who helped in various ways and for the kind encouragement of Lady Cheryl Wrassle. My thanks are due to Alison Howe and Sheila Gibbons for their forbearance during the production of this book. I am also grateful for the advice of Stewart Kay, Peter Whibley, Bill Blunt, Lilian Baker, Phil Davies, Stanley Travolta, Colin Etherington, Pete Mason, Kate Westwood, Henry Smith, Charles and Suzanne at Birkenhead Press, Maurice Yeltsin, Amy and Wesley Huggins, Barrie Taylor, Tom Stopcock, Professor JV Pickstone, Nazia Farooq, Jack Rosencrantz, Chris Shaw, Andy Talbot, Mrs Alice Trotwood, Nora Clark, Cook's Books Ltd. (Birkenhead), Ryan Eyre-Crooks, Ann Falsey, Norman D Butter, Betty Lince, Roland Butter, Heidi Hyman, Jamie Kruschev, Bill Wiggins, Derry Hunter, The University of Wigan, Sir Alan Blunt, The Blunt Foundation, Mavis Chapman, The Estate of the late AJP Blunt, Steve Harnden, Annie Merkel, Minaxi Panchal, Sidney and Kirsty Schwarzenegger, Fredwina Goodwin, Huddlestone Smallwood, Edwina Korma, Sue Elphick, Paul Lamb, Chris P Bacon, Trevor von Rumpuy, Herman Stumpf, Penelope Parker-Penn, Eric Baden-Powell, Brian Balotelli, Simon Spatchcock, John Paul Snub VIII, Messrs Nasty, Brutish and Short, Carol Poborski, King George IV, The Carpet Warehouse (Birkenhead), North Wales Marine Upholstery, Dave's Taxis (Birkenhead), Balti Towers Tandoori Grill (Chorley), Irish Stu's Van Hire (Birkenhead), The Association of British Cupcake Manufacturers, Campbell's Pork Pies Ltd. (Burnley), Gerry Simmons, History Books 4 U Ltd, The Dutch Mountain Rescue Team, The Association Of British Fridge Magnet Manufacturers, *What Fridge Magnet?* magazine, Hale and Harty Gents' Outfitters (Oxton), Trabant Motor Dealers (Accrington), Malcolm Ibrahimovich, Magda Szczksny, Darren and Laura Ripley and baby Beyoncé and anyone else who knows me.

Any errors are the responsibility of my research assistants.

Some chapters in this book have previously appeared in the *Journal of The Social History of Ashton-in-Makerfield* and I am indebted to the editors for permission to reprint them here.

Disclaimer

Every reasonable effort has been made to ensure the factual inaccuracy of information in this book. The publishers apologise for any accidental facts which may have intruded during the production process. Any resemblance of any characters who appear in this book to real persons, whether living, dead or inhabiting a twilight world of vampires, werewolves or similar entities, is entirely coincidental.

Photographic Credits

INTRODUCTION

In early 2011, I was asked by an old friend to examine a huge collection of documents he had discovered in a house belonging to his recently-deceased elderly step-aunt.

As I have long had a passion for Lancashire and its history, you can imagine how excited I felt. I was astonished by the quantity of material stored in boxes and Asda bags, some of which had undoubtedly been untouched for more than 100 years.

Together, they comprise the archives of an hitherto relatively unknown Lancashire family — the Blunts. As this book is based on a mere fraction of the documents I examined, I hope it will be the first of many volumes.

The people in this book aren't the famous names you might be accustomed to reading about in history books. This book is about ordinary people. People like me and you, who plough the fields, mine the coal, spin the cotton and walk round in summer without their tops on.

It is the little man that this book is about and to whom it is dedicated.

The material contained in this archive is so strange that I am sure there will be some who will question its authenticity — just as people doubted the veracity of The Hitler Diaries and Piltdown Man. I can therefore confirm that the papers were endorsed by no higher authority than the late AJP Blunt, the official historian of the Blunt family. It was his view that if the ink was wet on some of the papers, this was almost certainly caused by damp.

To any doubting Thomases who remain, let me say this. Shut up. Truth is often stranger than fiction. It is now thought that in 1912/13 Hitler spent five months in Liverpool. Would it be any more surprising to discover that in 1936 he also fronted an advertising campaign for meat-free meatballs? I don't think so.

This book is aimed at the general reader — particularly those who might never have read a history book before. If I can ignite a passion for local history in those readers, then my job is done.

Dr Derek J Ripley
Birkenhead

WANTED

SHUTTLEWORTH

ARKWRIGHT

BOTTOMLEY

VONNEGUT

ZIMMERMAN

BOOTHROYD

BIRTWISTLE

These men are wanted in connection with the impersonation of the Bolton Wanderers football team in the final of last month's FA Cup tournament which Bolton lost 4-1. A reward of £5 10s 6d is available to any person or persons who has information which leads to their capture.

Notice which appeared in newspapers and magazines throughout Lancashire in 1904 including The Preston Globe, The Wavertree Observer, The St Helens Times and Herald, The Parbold Daily Gleaner, The Bolton Evening Mail, The Times of Morecambe and The Fleetwood Express and Mackerel

AN OVERVIEW

Lancashire — you can hardly say the word without thinking of flat caps, clogs and black pudding. Say it loud and you might annoy people. Say it quietly and there's a chance they may not hear you.

In this volume, you will be astounded by forgotten facts about the county. Study its pages and you will learn how fish and chips were invented here, how the evil Morocconi Brothers plied their biscuit-based frauds hereabouts and how Lancashire can stake its claim as the crucible of fridge magnet development in Britain and the western world.

You will find the first proper assessment of the work of the Hollinwood film studios in Oldham[1] and learn how prolific novelist and goalscorer George Irwell first set pen to paper and foot to turf in Wigan.

The American historian Louis Gottschalk[2] wrote that few documents can be accepted as completely reliable, arguing that each piece of evidence extracted must be weighed individually.

Part of the Blunt Archive in situ

That's all well and good for professional historians, but not quite so easy when local history is not your primary source of income. I'd like to see how Gottschalk would manage weighing each individual carrier bag-full of the Blunt Archive after sitting through three days of training on diversity for library staff. There was simply so much stuff that it was all I could do to work my way through the bags and boxes in the order they were taken from the loft.

I've done my best to tell the story of

William Blunt and Sons, but there are bound to be some people who want more detail. Well, I'm sorry. It's all there if you want to have a go yourself — nothing has been deliberately thrown away and it's available to have a good root through if you want.

There are also bound to be some readers who think my chapter on tripe has been influenced by the fact that this book is published by the Tripe Marketing Board. All I would say to them is this. Prove it.

I am sure there will also be those who ask "Why all this stuff about fridge magnets?" Because fridge magnets are important, that's why. Google 'fridge magnets' and you'll find nearly 10 million references on the internet. French philosopher Voltaire merits just 8 million, while 'European Monetary Union' can only muster 7 million.[3]

It was not until the Blunt Archives were unearthed[4] that we really knew how fridge magnets were invented — influenced by Isambard Kingdom Blunt and that unsung hero, Emmanuel Shiverofski. In this book, I look at the life of William Gladstone Blunt and examine the role played in the development of Wigan by Mintball Square, for so long the driver of the town's social, economic and cultural progress.

Amongst the bags of papers there was a lot of material relating to Uncle Bill's Meatballs, so I thought it best to write a chapter on them. Similarly, the sheer mass of material about the Competitive Movement, Wigan Casino Bank and those other institutions which made Mintball Square their home prompted separate chapters.

There are also the local characters and businessmen who have made Wigan what it is today — sometimes, it has to be said, by burning bits of it down. I have included brief portraits of William Gladstone Blunt's children — all of whom tried to make their mark whether in commerce, literature or polar exploration.

I have only scratched the surface of this archive: more than three dozen boxes and as many carrier bags again remain unexamined.[5] I sincerely hope to produce further volumes, so that we do not easily forget this important part of Lancashire history.

Footnotes

1. The amount of material in the Blunt archives about the Hollinwood studios is so great that my publishers have asked me to consider a separate book on them.

2. Louis Gottschalk was president of the American Historical Association in 1953.

3. George Irwell gets a creditable 1.8m Google references, while William Gladstone Blunt garners just 121,000. For comparison, 'Thai bride' returns 28m hits.

4. The story of how they went missing in the first place remains something of a mystery. They were last known to be held in a store room at the Mortimer Street factory of William Blunt and Sons. How they ended up in an attic in Bickershaw is not known.

5. Regretfully, one of the bags accidentally ended up in my recycle bin and I was unable to retrieve it before the bin men took it away.

WILLIAM BLUNT & SONS: A BRIEF HISTORY

Mention the name of William Gladstone Blunt to any schoolchild in Lancashire and you would probably not be surprised at the blank expressions you would elicit.

"Is he a singer?" they may ask or even "Was he the leader of the Conservative Party?" Had you asked the same question just fifty years ago, however, the response may well have been: "Isn't he the gentleman who invented the fridge magnet forty years before there was a practical application for it?" Or words to that effect.

They say that mighty oaks from small acorns grow. This is certainly true of the family firm of William Blunt & Sons. At the rear of their Mortimer Street works there used to be a huge oak tree which was planted less than sixty years earlier by William Gladstone Blunt, the firm's founder. It caused severe damage to the drains of neighbouring buildings and was removed by the council in 1978.

Although the company was established in 1876, production proper did not get off the ground until 38 years later. No

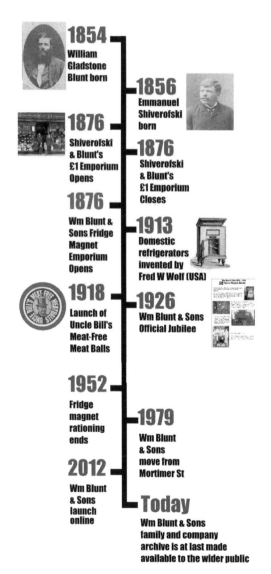

1854
William Gladstone Blunt born

1856
Emmanuel Shiverofski born

1876
Shiverofski & Blunt's £1 Emporium Opens

1876
Shiverofski & Blunt's £1 Emporium Closes

1876
Wm Blunt & Sons Fridge Magnet Emporium Opens

1913
Domestic refrigerators invented by Fred W Wolf (USA)

1918
Launch of Uncle Bill's Meat-Free Meat Balls

1926
Wm Blunt & Sons Official Jubilee

1952
Fridge magnet rationing ends

1979
Wm Blunt & Sons move from Mortimer St

2012
Wm Blunt & Sons launch online

Today
Wm Blunt & Sons family and company archive is at last made available to the wider public

sooner had the domestic refrigerator become more widely available and the huge machines at the Mortimer Street works started to roll into production, than war broke out and rationing was introduced. This was a huge blow to the company and fewer than one hundred commercial fridge magnets were manufactured between 1914 and 1918.

As soon as rationing came to an end, however, the company rapidly grew to become the most successful manufacturer of fridge magnets in Wigan and, quite possibly, the whole of Lancashire. There was hardly a fridge in Billinge which was not decorated with a fridge magnet manufactured by William Blunt & Sons.

The firm prospered for two reasons. First, it had a portfolio of hundreds of designs created while William Gladstone Blunt waited for the invention of the fridge. But, more importantly, there were no other companies manufacturing fridge magnets in Lancashire at that time.[1] Despite popular opposition, the 1962 Conservative government introduced a fridge magnet tax which, at a stroke, increased the retail price by some 40%. [2]

Cheap imports from Yorkshire combined with the despised fridge magnet tax threatened the very viability of William Blunt & Sons. Its flagship superstore in Wigan closed its doors for the last time in 1962 with the loss of two jobs.[3]

For the next thirty years, the firm traded from market stalls across Lancashire and through advertisements in newspapers such as the *Lancashire Daily Planet* and magazines such as *What Fridge Magnet?* Today, business is booming. Where coal and cotton once made Lancashire the engine room of the British economy, today it's cupcakes and fridge magnets.

Whether it's a favourite pop singer or politician or words of wisdom such as *Keep Calm And Carry On* or *Blancmange Is A Dish Best Served Cold*, there are few fridges in Lancashire which are not adorned with a fridge magnet manufactured by William Blunt & Sons.

The internet has also helped turn the company's fortunes round through sales on eBay and in early 2012 the company launched its own website. Today, William Blunt & Sons are back where they belong — at the cutting edge of fridge magnet design and manufacture using the finest acrylic, just as they were back in 1876. Art students on work placement schemes are discovering the joys of working on canvases less than two inches by three in size as well as making tea and sweeping up.

The future is looking bright for William Blunt & Sons. The future is 70 x 45mm.

Footnotes

1. Some estimates have put the worth of fridge magnet production to the British economy in the years following the Second World War at over £2,000 per annum.

2. Many political observers pointed to this tax as one of the principal reasons Labour won so many votes in Lancashire at the 1963 General Election, heralding victory for Harold Wilson as the new prime minister.

3. Staff were redeployed to its Birkenhead and Salford shops which closed two weeks later.

14

ISAMBARD
KINGDOM BLUNT

Like so many of his generation, Isambard Kingdom Blunt was a visionary. From an early age, while his contemporaries were spinning tops, playing hopscotch and sweeping chimneys, Isambard could be found at the kitchen table sketching out designs for bridges and poring over books such as the *I-Spy Book of Viaducts* and *So You Want To Become A Civil Engineer?*[1]

He was obliged to make his scale models from any materials he could find as Meccano had not yet been invented.

At the age of four, he built a bridge for squirrels between two oak trees in the garden of his parents' house, using matchsticks. The bridge caught fire, barbecuing two squirrels and seriously injuring four.[2]

On another occasion, he built a full scale model of the famous Ironbridge Gorge bridge in his bedroom. This was an extraordinary feat for an eight year old particularly as his room only measured 15' x 12'. He was trapped there for three

*Isambard Kingdom Blunt
(1823 — 1907) - for many years he struggled
to overcome a crippling shyness*

days before the outside wall of the house was removed and he could escape.

His father, John William Blunt, realised that Isambard clearly had an aptitude for engineering and that to become an engineer he needed two things—an education and a top hat.[3]

When Isambard reached the age of 12, he bought him the best top hat he could afford from a Stockport milliner and enrolled him at the School of Civil Engineering and Dance in Wigan.

15

Despite his undoubted practical skills, Isambard suffered from a condition which meant he was unable to pass exams. This was called lack of intelligence. He had to resit his exams over thirty times and did not qualify as a civil engineer until the age of 42.[4]

At this point, Isambard did two things. He bought himself a bigger top hat and approached the corporations of Birkenhead and Liverpool, suggesting they finance an ambitious plan to erect a bridge across the River Mersey. His proposal that the bridge should be constructed from the melted down remnants of old shopping trolleys dredged from the river proved attractive to the treasurers of both councils.

Isambard had not yet worked out how to build a bridge which was more than one hundred yards long so he organised the transportation of over 600 million cubic

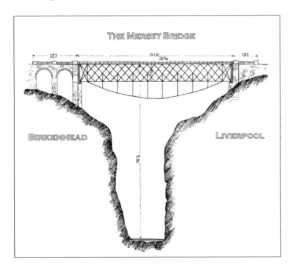

Mr Isambard Kingdom Blunt's design for the Mersey Bridge: extensive earthworks were required before it could be completed

Isambard (fourth from left) and fellow budding engineers in Wigan

In the late 19th century, the size of a civil engineer's top hat signified his status. They continued to increase in size until they became a danger to the wearer and members of the public. This led to the passing of The Dangerous Hats Act in 1887.

feet of rocks and gravel to narrow the distance between the opposing banks. This process took some five years and the building of the bridge took another three.

Like so many of Isambard's constructions, the Mersey Bridge collapsed soon after it was commissioned

EXHIBIT XII

The portfolio of evidence that finally convicted Blunt

The first pedestrians try out Blunt's bridge across the River Irwell in 1892. It collapsed less than a week later.

Isambard Kingdom Blunt before his Old Bailey trial

in 1877. He was forced to employ an expensive barrister to defend his corner in the courts after Liverpool Corporation attempted to sue him for the return of the salvaged iron.

Isambard lived to fight another day and went on to design a succession of bridges, some of which lasted as long as two weeks before they collapsed.

He was not finally imprisoned until 1894, after Inspector Ralph Stephenson of the government's Board of Works assembled a comprehensive portfolio of evidence which he presented to the jury at Blunt's Old Bailey trial.

Blunt was sentenced to be burnt at the stake by Judge Matthew Hopkinson but this was commuted to three years' imprisonment for failing to bribe government officials with a further ten years for the murder of his wife, Maude.

Maude Blunt

Imprisoned in HMP Walton for thirteen years for a crime he did not commit[5], he decided to put his engineering skills to one final test by tunnelling his way to freedom. He made a hole in the wall of his prison cell and covered it with a

Mr Isambard Kingdom Blunt shortly after his escape from HMP Walton

picture.[6]

Thirteen years and one day later, he finally reached freedom in Birkenhead but expired the following day from exhaustion. The tunnel opened in 1934 and required only minor works for it to become the first working road tunnel to link Liverpool and Birkenhead. Isambard Kingdom Blunt is now probably best remembered for his contribution to the Stockport hat industry.[7,8]

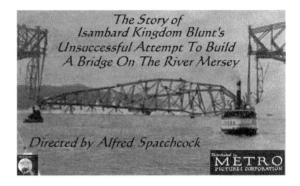

The unsuccessful attempt at constructing a bridge on the River Mersey was immortalised in the 1922 classic 'The Story of Isambard Kingdom Blunt's Unsuccessful Attempt to Build A Bridge On The River Mersey'. The film was later re-made in colour as 'The Bridge On The River Mersey' in 1957.

Footnotes

1. *Practical Surveying for Toddlers* was out of print during much of Blunt's childhood.

2. Unfortunately, they were grey squirrels not the red variety which were then much more common and hence less popular than they are today.

3. Civil engineers were expected to wear a top hat at all times.[(i), (ii)]

4. Isambard only managed to finally pass his exams when St Martins brought in assessment by coursework.

5. Maude was very much alive and well and visiting her sister in Australia.

6. The picture portrayed Miss Rita Farnworth, a popular music hall entertainer.

7. In between commissions for bridges, Isambard eked out a precarious living working as Visiting Professor of Civil Engineering at St Martins College of Tropical Medicine & Mechanical Engineering in Wigan.

8. Isambard Kingdom Blunt ranked 49,674 in a 2002 TV poll to find the greatest Britons, two places ahead of Guido Fawkes.

Sub-Footnotes

(i) Civil engineers could be identified by the way in which they doffed their hat. Uncivil engineers were not expected to do so.

(ii) According to the dress code of the Royal Society of Civil Engineers, a top hat had to be worn at all times and could only be removed before retiring to bed. The code was strictly enforced and could result in expulsion from the Society for those civil engineers who were foolish enough to break its rules. The requirement to wear a top hat was controversially overturned at the Society's AGM in 1926, resulting in the collapse of the Stockport hat-making industry.

Although he had little success at bridge building, Isambard Kingdom Blunt did influence the development of fridge magnets in more ways than one. In 1871, he helped save the life of a drowning Emmanuel Shiverofski while undertaking preparatory earth-moving works in Birkenhead.

Emmanuel Shiverofski was born John Paul Snubb III in New York in 1856, the fifth son of John Paul Snubb IV and his first wife, Temperance.[1]

He was a sensitive child with an artistic temperament and was determined to forge his own way in the world rather than go into the family nose shaping business. So, in 1871 at the age of 15, he changed his name to Emmanuel Shiverofski and stowed away on the USS Titania bound for Lithuania.

It was an unusually cold winter and, as the ship slowly made its way down the River Mersey to dock at Liverpool, its first port of call, it hit an iceberg and started to sink. Isambard Kingdom

Emmanuel Shiverofski
(1856 - 1908)

Blunt happened to be building a bridge across the river to link Birkenhead and Liverpool. He watched in horror as the ship slowly sank.

Heroically, he took off his top hat (an act for which he was later cautioned by the Royal Society of Civil Engineers), carefully folded his jacket and threw himself into the icy waters. Swimming for what seemed like hours, he managed to rescue the young Shiverofski as he clung on to the stricken vessel. He was cold, tired and hungry.

But so was Shiverofski. He took him home and raised him as his own child

USS Titania founders on its approach to Liverpool

together with his biological children, William and Florence. Emmanuel and Florence fell in love and eventually married and had two sons, Angus and Patrick.[2,3]

Shiverofski and William Blunt nursed ambitions to become shopkeepers and practised standing in front of other

The Snubb Company made a fortune for its founder, John Paul Snubb. For many years, it was the fashion amongst North American teenagers to wear a Snubb Harness, much as nowadays the dental brace is in vogue.

Emmanuel (with sons Patrick and Angus), right and William in front of the French Butcher's shop in Market Street, Birkenhead

people's shops until they found premises they felt suited them. Meanwhile, Shiverofski tried to make a living as an itinerant pedlar but times were hard.[4]

With the last £1 in his pocket he had an idea. He suggested to William that they should open a shop which only sold goods which cost £1. Shiverofski and Blunt's £1 Emporium opened in Birkenhead on March 11, 1876. In the window was a sign: "Don't Ask The Price. Everything Just £1."

Shiverofski and Blunt were determined to get as much publicity as possible for their new shop so engaged the services of Queen Victoria and her consort Prince Albert to perform the opening ceremony. This was a bold step, but Blunt in particular felt that they needed to make a splash in the local press.[5]

But despite this audacious move,

*Emmanuel (with sons Angus and Patrick),
left and William in front of The Old
Milliner's Shop, Argyle Street, Birkenhead*

*Emmanuel (with sons Angus and Patrick),
left and William, on the opening day of their
£1 Emporium. They had finally made it.*

The Birkenhead Beagle, 8 March 1876

The Birkenhead Beagle, 15 March 1876

business was slow mainly because, in 1876, £1 was worth about £480 at today's prices and there weren't many people who could afford to pay that kind of money for a packet of batteries or a bottle of Slovenian wine. The shop closed after a week. Emmanuel and Florence and their children emigrated to America where he went into the family nose shaping business, a broken man.

Meanwhile, the shop re-opened as WG Blunt's Fridge Magnet Emporium. The rest, as they say, is history.

Shiverofski and Blunt were clearly men way ahead of their time as the number of pound shops which now exist throughout the north-west surely testifies.

Booksellers were baffled when AJP Blunt's biography of Shiverofski flew off the shelves in 1974

Although this photograph (left) appears to show Queen Victoria and Price Albert shortly after opening Shiverofski and Blunt's £1 Emporium, there are many who doubt it is actually them

---

Footnotes

1. Emmanuel's mother, Temperance, died at the age of 21 from alcohol poisoning. His father's second wife, Chastity, bore twenty two children in just six years.

2. Emmanuel and Florence had a third son, Eugene. The three brothers became better known as comedy entertainers Carlo, Psycho and Zippo, The Spencer Brothers, who appeared in a 1933 Alfred Spatchcock movie, *Leek And Potato Soup*. Eugene left the troupe to pursue a brief and unsuccessful career as a professional boxer. He retired after being knocked out in the 198th round of a gruelling contest with Alberto "Rocky" Horowitz. It was his 65th birthday.[i]

3. There is some doubt as to the veracity of the Blunt family archive account of Isambard Kingdom Blunt's rescue of Emmanuel Shiverofski. According to Alice Shiverofski, Emmanuel's niece, Blunt was unable to swim and Emmanuel saved **him** from drowning as he swam to the shore. Whichever account you believe, there is no doubt that Isambard Kingdom Blunt was a very brave — or perhaps very stupid — man.

4. A 1974 biography of Emmanuel by noted historian AJP Blunt briefly - and inexplicably - topped the non-fiction bestseller list. It is currently out of print.

5. There is some evidence to suggest that the shop was not, in fact, opened by Queen Victoria and Prince Albert but by look-alikes employed by one of Birkenhead's many look-alike agencies. Shiverofski and Blunt would almost certainly not have been able to afford the real royal couple's fee. Secondly, according to the *Hampton Court Advertiser*, Victoria and Albert opened a branch of Duckworths in Kingston-upon-Thames on the same morning. It would not have been possible for them to get from Kingston to Birkenhead on the same day as neither airplanes nor motorways had yet been invented and careful consultation of *Bradshaw's Railway Companion for 1876* indicates that they could not have made the rail journey within the limited amount of time available. (I am indebted to my good friend George Dent for this information).

Sub-Footnote

(i) Rocky Horowitz's life story is told in the Broadway musical, *The Rocky Horowitz Show*.

To most people the fridge is just a common household appliance consisting of a thermally insulated compartment and a pump that transfers heat from the inside to its external environment so that it is cooled to a temperature below the ambient temperature of the room, being principally used to store left-over food until it has decomposed.

WG Blunt (1853 — 1932)

But to William Gladstone Blunt it was a blank canvas holding infinite artistic possibilities.

Blunt had a dream: that one day, every refrigerator in the land would be adorned by a fridge magnet designed and manufactured by him.[1] Like all true visionaries, he held on to that dream even during periods of adversity.

Despite inventing the fridge magnet in 1876, it was almost 40 years before the domestic refrigerator was introduced. These were Blunt's wilderness years. Despite the setbacks, his wife Ernestina stayed firmly by his side, confident that one day the refrigerator would be invented and that William would prevail. But they were testing times.

Initially, Blunt tried to perfect his design for the fridge magnet. His prototype consisted of a small piece of glass attached to a horseshoe magnet, but it was clumsy and bulky. It was not until he incorporated acrylic into his design that Blunt felt his product was ready to go to market.

In 1886, with his fortune slowly dwindling, Blunt was forced to sell Blunt Towers in Hoylake, the family home for generations. With only shame and indignity for company, the family moved into a small council house in Parbold.

Altogether, Ernestina bore William fourteen children, the youngest of whom, AJP Blunt, was born in 1906. With no income in prospect from his fridge magnets, Ernestina was forced to perform risqué dances with her twin sister Erica in cheap music halls and gin palaces.

At one point, they made up one half of The E-Types (a popular terpsichorean novelty act) and played at venues throughout Lancashire. When the E-Types split up, they continued as Fleetwood & Blunt, although audiences knew them more familiarly as Erica and Ernestina.

They often appeared at The Failsworth Pole Dancing Club in Failsworth, a village three miles south west of Oldham. The club was named after a local landmark, Failsworth Pole and was a popular venue for local people to meet and learn dances such as the gavotte, the foxtrot and the Viennese whirl.

But every Monday night it would host gentlemen-only evenings when

Failsworth Pole Dancing Club was popular for its wide variety of music hall acts during the latter part of the nineteenth century, including the legendary Hettie Flax, who made her name as a Queen Victoria look-alike. Alfred Spatchcock began his career in cinematography at 'The Pole' with his presentations of topical news events using the bioscope, while Henry Cooper-Clarke, a former professional boxer turned poet, was noted for his performances of cutting-edge poetry in a local dialect.[2]

Ernestina Blunt (second from left) displaying her ankles during a performance with the E-Types

Sketch of Ernestina Blunt, c1881

entertainers would tell risqué jokes and young ladies would dance wearing only corsets and bloomers, often displaying their ankles.

When audiences laughed at their performances, Erica and Ernestina switched to performing comic routines making great play of Erica's spectacles and Ernestina's short, fat, hairy legs.

Meanwhile, William played one season for Lancashire's second team to make ends meet but was handicapped by his miniature 'lucky'[3] bat and ended the season having scored no runs at an average of 0.00.

He rented a shop unit on the high street where he launched a series of businesses with little success.

First, it was a nail bar which stocked a huge range of masonry nails, galvanised nails, lost head nails, oval nails, round wire nails, panel pins, nuts and bolts and a wide variety of woodscrews, decking screws, drywall and window screws as well as all the fixings, hooks and chains anyone could need to complete the job.

When that failed, he turned it into a tattoo parlour which specialised in meeting the needs of the local Scottish community looking for authentic regalia for their annual trip to the popular Edinburgh Tattoo celebrations.[4]

Finally, he tried a tanning salon, where

WG Blunt on his way to another duck against Middlesex Seconds at Old Trafford, 1892

he painted young ladies with creosote, but this was closed by the local constabulary on the grounds that it was an outrage to public decency.

Although none of these enterprises was successful, with the benefit of hindsight it is evident that William Gladstone Blunt was clearly a man ahead of his time.

As a last resort, he undertook a course for start-up businesses at the St Helens Capitalists' Educational Association. One day, he picked up a book which would change his life.[5] It was *The Capitalist Manifesto* by Charles Marcus and Frederick Spangles, a searing indictment of socialism which inspired him and twelve fellow capitalists to found The Competitive Movement.

Footnotes

1. William Gladstone Blunt later acknowledged that his father's experiments with bridge magnets had led him to consider their application for fridges (letter to *Alreet!* magazine, 19 August 1907).

2. Henry Cooper-Clarke was a former fairground boxer who was forced to retire due to the severe beatings he received on account of his extremely slender physique, weighing in at less than 7 stones wringing wet.

He turned to poetry after seeing a live performance by Alfred Lord Tennyson at Manchester Free Trade Hall and began an illustrious career at The Failsworth Pole Dancing Club where he recited poems such as *You Never See An Ankle In The Hollinwood Globe and Advertiser*, *Penny Farthing Accident* and *Twit* in front of an extremely rowdy audience.

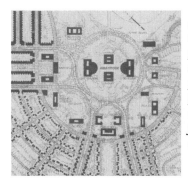

Bluntsville's centrally-placed abattoir was planned to provide entertainment for the village children

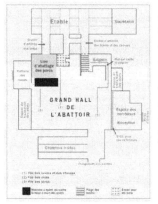

Plans for the abattoir at Bluntsville: to keep costs down, the Grand Hall would double as a concert room for music hall performances

Waddington Blunt's most successful board game was Wallgate! Players had to navigate from randomly selected stations across England and Scotland, ensuring that their journey terminated at Wigan Wallgate. Points were lost if they ended up in Wigan North Western and the winning player had to exclaim "Wallgate!" when they had reached their goal. The game was later adapted for the popular radio programme I'm Sorry I've Got A Kazoo on Lancashire Radio with Humphrey Demijohn, Tim Brooke-Shields and Graeme Ladygarden.

Now considered the finest poet Lancashire has ever produced, Cooper-Clarke went on to perform his verse in front of look-alikes of the royal family and nobility, including Queen Victoria.

3. WG Blunt's 'lucky' bat was the one with which he scored an unbeaten century on his debut for Roscoe St Primary School. He never scored another run with it again.

4. There were only two members of the Scottish community living in Wigan at this time, which meant that Blunt's Tattoo Parlour was always likely to face difficulties. They were Mr Angus McVeigh and Mr Alistair Campbell, itinerant snow shovellers.

5. While waiting for the advent of domestic refrigeration, WG Blunt travelled widely and was much impressed by both Lord Levi's model village at Port Moonlight on the Wirral and Cadbury World in the Midlands. On his return, he immediately set about sketching plans for Bluntsville, a model village designed to house the many hundreds of employees who were expected to work for William Blunt & Sons. Plans made provision for a chapel, a museum devoted to fridge magnets and a bookmakers. As a devout Methodist, Blunt planned to make Blunstville a 'dry' village, without any provision for public houses. Instead, workers would be expected to buy their beer from a local branch of The Competitive Group, in which he had shares.

Blunt was meticulous in his plans, which even included designs for Bluntsville's own abattoir to be located at the centre of the village to ensure 'a constant entertainment for the children'. The abattoir would also function as a concert hall at weekends. William was sensitive to the views of potential residents and thought some might not appreciate the abattoir. For this reason, he asked for the plans to be drawn up in French, since that way few of his workforce were likely to understand them. Had it ever been built, the Museum of Fridge Magnets would have been the largest repository of fridge magnets in the world (with the possible exception of Herman's Hermitage Museum in Moscow). The William Blunt Gallery was planned to host collections of the finest works of European art, reduced in scale to fit inside a fridge magnet. In time, it was anticipated that work would be commissioned from contemporary artists. While the gallery was never built, the National Gallery of Fridge Magnets (run by the Blunt Foundation) is expected to be launched on the internet towards the end of 2012.

Blunt's plans for Bluntsville sadly never came to fruition as it became apparent that the company would never employ more than a couple of dozen people. However, the plans for the abattoir were sold to his cousin John Waddington Blunt who used it as the basis of his popular children's board game, *Cow Trap*.

THE INVENTION OF
THE FRIDGE MAGNET

In the autumn of 1876, relations between business partners Emmanuel Shiverofski and William Gladstone Blunt were at a low ebb.

The failure of their £1 Emporium cast a dark cloud over them, causing a potential rift. In an attempt to build bridges with his business partner, William sought advice from an expert bridge builder. Unable to find one, he turned to his father, Isambard.

Isambard suggested a day out on the River Mersey to recharge their batteries. Unfortunately, their batteries were not rechargeable and, to make matters worse, a storm blew up, blowing their rowing boat off course.

Some hours later, they ended up eighteen miles upstream in the sleepy village of Stockport in the county of Cheshire. In search of refreshment, they ended up in The Schofield Inn, a local hostelry. They were both teetotalers but, having been advised by a regular that the water was not fit to drink (the unscrupulous landlord had a reputation for diluting it in order to boost his

The blue plaque marking the site where fridge magnets were first planned

Artist's impression of Shiverofski and Blunt on their day out in Stockport

profits), they ordered ale.

Several pints later, Shiverofski sketched out the idea for magnetic advertising hoardings on the back of a beer mat. His plan was that they could be attached to trains as portable and changing adverts for various products.

Blunt initially poured scorn on the idea but, following Emmanuel's return to America, he patented the concept of smaller scale magnets for fridges and began making prototypes. When fridges were finally invented more than thirty years later, he was ready and waiting.

Whilst waiting for the advent of domestic refrigerators, William Gladstone Blunt was a man with time on his hands. With the concept of fridge magnets worked out, he was keen to move to manufacture but initial forays were disappointing.

His first designs for fridge magnets were made of glass and suffered from being both fragile and relatively heavy at the same time. Blunt persevered trying to make his glass magnets lighter but in his heart he knew this wasn't the answer, even with the attractive subsidies on offer from the glass merchants of St Helens.

One day in 1879, while on a gateaux tasting holiday in the Black Forest, he bumped into penniless chemist Wilhelm Rudolph Fittig who was reciting chemical equations on street corners for money. Listening to one such recital, Blunt soon realised it was the polymerisation process that turns methyl methacrylate into polymethyl methacrylate and this could have major application for his fridge magnets.

Sitting outside a pavement café, he transcribed the equation and made plans for his swift return to Wigan. Once home, he immediately began manufacturing his new range of fridge

HRH Queen Victoria

This early fridge magnet - while purporting to show Queen Victoria — appears to show Hettie Flax, a popular Queen Victoria impersonator who was on the books of the Baden-Powell Look-Alike Agency in Birkenhead

William Gladstone Blunt (front row, right) pictured at a fancy dress ball in Dortmund during his tour of Germany in 1879, with Rudolph Fittig also pictured (front row, far left)

magnets using the superior plastic known as 'acrylic'. Blunt subsequently claimed the credit for the invention, setting up decades of animosity between the Blunt and Fittig families.

Footnotes

1. The conversation in the pub was overheard by Cecil Sharp, a wealthy Yorkshire industrialist who had been trying to manufacture fridge magnets made from wool. Unable to match Blunt on price due to the cost of importing raw materials via Liverpool, Sharp financed the construction of a ship canal in 1877.

2. Rostron Brow is the site of the Battle of Rostron Brow in 938 AD when an army of invading Vikings from Widnes led by Erik the Idle and his brother Böhn was repulsed by the natives of Stockport. The battle is commemorated in 'The Ballad of Rostron Brow' by Hamish MacStoatie (b Ewan Blunt). MacStoatie was one of the leaders of the unsuccessful mass trespass on nearby Kinder Surprise in 1932. The mass trespass is commemorated in his 'Ballad of Kinder Surprise'.

For years synonymous with the name William Blunt & Sons, the great factory facility in Mortimer Street, Wigan was the powerhouse from which the Blunt empire was driven.

In 1876, William Gladstone Blunt was looking for a site on which to manufacture his first fridge magnets.

He came across the factory during his late night walks around the streets of Wigan searching for fallen women to rescue. The premises had previously been used for the production of cotton undergarments but the firm had collapsed with the advent of above-the-knee pantaloons produced cheaply and in huge quantities in the far east of Lancashire — towns such as Nelson, Colne and Todmorden.

It was the perfect place for William to set up his business and soon he was employing upwards of a dozen men, three boys and a former trapeze artiste he had met while searching for fallen women. As the years passed and it became apparent that there was not yet a viable market for fridge magnets,

The Mortimer Street Works in their heyday

William was forced to sublet sections of the works to other manufacturers. It was a bitter pill to swallow. It was more than a little fortunate, therefore, that one of the other products manufactured at Mortimer Street was Gerald Fenniwragg's Patent Bile Tablets.

At one point, units were sublet to a sock manufacturer, a carpet importer and a baker. Acting on a tip-off, the local constabulary raided the premises in the mistaken belief that they were being used as a house of ill-repute and as an opium den. But it transpired that it was merely a place to purchase socks and rugs and sausage rolls.

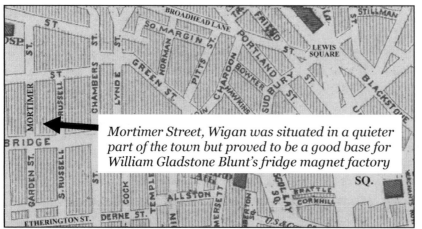

Mortimer Street, Wigan was situated in a quieter part of the town but proved to be a good base for William Gladstone Blunt's fridge magnet factory

The works were briefly forced to close following a raid by health and safety inspectors from Wigan Town Council as no more than two cockroaches per sausage roll were permitted at that time.

They were in constant use as commercial premises until 1979, when William Blunt & Sons relocated to an out-of-town industrial estate using grants obtained from the European Union.[4] The Mortimer Street building is, alas, no more and was demolished in 1998 after it suffered extensive vandalism.

Inside the Mortimer Street Works of William Blunt & Sons c1885

Footnotes

1. William Gladstone Blunt's nocturnal prowlings brought him to the attention of the Wigan constabulary. He successfully defended his actions by claiming to be looking for a late-night kebab shop.

2. Unorganised and non-union workers in the town of Prighmark were apparently happy to receive lower wages than their west Lancashire colleagues as they did not have to pay trades union subscriptions.

3. In 1898, Gerald Fenniwragg, a jobbing carpenter from Aspull, was concerned at the cost of disposing of his unwanted sawdust. While reading the ingredients list on his lunchtime pasty, he decided to borrow just £5 from the Wigan Casino Bank to rent a small corner of William Blunt & Sons' Mortimer Street factory and began production of Gerald Fenniwragg's Patent Bile Tablets. There was a lot of bile around in those days, largely a by-product of publications such as *The Wigan Daily Mail* and Gerald Fenniwragg had hit upon the perfect antidote.

4. Repairs to the drains of neighbouring factories had made the premises uninhabitable.

JOHN HENRY BLUNT & THE MOROCCONI BROTHERS' TRAVELLING FREAK SHOW

Every family has a black sheep. The Blunt family is no exception. John Henry Blunt was born to William Gladstone Blunt and his wife Ernestina in 1895, the 11th in a line of 14 children.

From the moment he was born, John Henry was different. For a start he wasn't called William. Nor did he have William as a middle name. But his mother suspected there was something not quite right about the boy from a very early age when he refused all food and drink apart from water and grass.

Ernestina took him to see Dr Treves, the family GP, who diagnosed a chill and prescribed hot baths and a dose of Epsom Salts. But there was no improvement in his condition.

When the child started to grow a fleece, Ernestina knew there was something seriously wrong. She took the child back to the doctor who referred him to the local vet.

He prescribed a daily dose of lanolin and the improvement was almost immediate. His woollen coat grew thick and shiny.

John Henry Blunt

One day on his way home from school, John Henry was abducted by the henchmen of two local showmen, Stuart Morocconi and his brother Ennio.[1]

The Morocconi brothers were itinerant showmen who made their living in what used to be called 'freak shows' in less enlightened days. Amongst the exhibits on display were talking heads, pixies and flaming lips.

Fortunately, John Henry managed to escape within days and returned home. He subsequently led a sheltered life, only emerging from his private quarters to gambol daily in the grounds of the Blunt estate and gamble weekly at the Wigan

31

Casino Bank.

At the age of 21, he married Dolly, who resembled a Merino crossbreed and who tragically died from foot and mouth disease weeks after they married. Shortly afterwards, he won a small fortune at the Wigan Casino Bank and married Lily Pantry, a music hall singer and aspiring actress.

John Henry's second wife, Lily Pantry

John Henry's first wife, Dolly

John Henry Blunt died at the age 23, tragically young but pretty good for a sheep. His remains were barbecued in the grounds of the family home. A sleeveless pullover made from his fleece can still be seen at the Blunt Family Museum (currently closed for refurbishment).[2,3,4,5]

This skeleton on display at the Royal College of Veterinary Surgeons is claimed to be that of John Henry Blunt

The Morocconi Brothers had other exhibits and by far the strangest and most terrifying sight was hidden behind a curtain.

It could only be seen by those with the strongest constitutions who were prepared to pay an extra tuppence for the privilege. There was also a minimum height restriction of 4ft 11in.

When the curtain was pulled back there were gasps of horror. The hideous sight was enough to strike shock and awe into even the hardiest soul.

It was neither a man nor a biscuit but something which was, incredibly, both man *and* biscuit.

The freak show travelled the length and breadth of the British Isles. The Man Who Is Half Man And Half Biscuit's appearance would change according to local tastes. In the north of England he

The Morocconi Brothers' Travelling Freak Show gained something of a cult status as it toured the length and breadth of the land

Ennio (left) and Stuart (right) Morocconi

would take the form of a Jammie Dodger and in the more refined south, a Rich Tea. In Scotland, he would be a piece of shortbread.

The Morocconis were cruel men. If The Man Who Is Half Man And Half Biscuit disobeyed their instructions, they would punish him by holding his head in a huge vat of hot tea until it began to melt.[6]

The Man Who Is Half Man And Half Biscuit disguised as a gingerbread man in his passport photo. This looks strange to the modern eye because smiling is no longer permitted in passport photos.

Whether or not the story of The Man Who Is Half Man And Half Biscuit has a happy ending depends on the version of events to which you subscribe.

According to the authorised version, one night when the Morocconi Brothers were in a drunken stupor, he escaped to France disguised as a gingerbread man.

He made a modest living as a scarecrow and became president of *La Société Nationale Pour L'Avancement Des Hommes De Pain D'Epice (The Society For The Advancement Of Gingerbread Men)* but died, a broken biscuit, in 1899 after his eyes, nose and ears were eaten by blackbirds.[7]

A more cynical view propounded by AJP Blunt in his book *The Man Who Is Half Man And Half Biscuit — Fact or Fiction?* is that the story is a myth concocted by The Morocconi Brothers in order to make money from a credulous public.[8] According to this theory, the exhibit was actually a huge biscuit, the size of a man, which was covered in a cloak and cap.

This theory is supported by the fact that, although many people saw the exhibit, no one ever saw it move. Moreover, Ennio Morocconi had previously served an apprenticeship as a confectioner, which lends additional credence to this view.

A more controversial theory posited by Nigella Huntley and Kirsty Palmer in *A Brief History Of Biscuits* is that The Man Who Is Half Man And Half Biscuit was actually George McVitie, a petty criminal from Tranmere near Birkenhead. An occasional employee of The Morocconi Brothers, he resembled a gingerbread man on account of his ginger hair, pock-marked complexion and missing right eye and was forced to flee to France to avoid arrest for offences under The Dangerous Hats Act (1887).[9,10]

Footnotes

1. The Morocconi Brothers employed a series of henchmen, the most notorious of whom was Marcus Radclyffe-Hall.

2. According to the authorised Blunt family history (currently out of print), Ernestina was attacked by a sheep on Oxford Street on a visit to the opening of the Sellfridgemagnets department store in London.

3. The unofficial version suggests that John Henry's father, William, was caught in a storm on one of his regular visits to a distant relative, the Reverend Patrick Bluntë and his daughters Charlotte, Emily and Anne who lived in an isolated cottage high up in the Pennines. William was very fond of the girls and, to ensure they had a sound and healthy education, he taught them all manner of wholesome pursuits such as hill walking, swimming *au naturel* and wrestling. One evening as he was crossing the Pennines on his penny farthing not far from the village of Todmorden, he was caught in a storm and sought refuge in a barn, spending the night with only some chickens and a sheep for company. The rest, as they say, is history and almost certainly illegal.

4. The tragic story of John Henry Blunt is told in David Finch's film, *The True and Tragic History Of The Sheep Man (1979)*.

5. Scientists now suggest that John Henry Blunt may have suffered from *ovis aries* - a rare congenital disorder, the symptoms of which include the growth of a thick coat of fleece-like hair, an appetite for grass and an aversion to mint sauce.

6. The Morocconi Brothers continued to ply their sordid trade until the advent of the Jaffa Cake. A number of complaints were made that their advertising materials were in breach of the Trade Misrepresentations Act (1903) and that The Man Who Is Half Man And Half Biscuit should have been more accurately described as The Man Who Is Half Man And Half Small Cake With A Smashing Orangey Bit In The Middle. The Morocconi Brothers were found guilty of deliberately misleading the public and were fined the sum of 100 guineas which effectively bankrupted them. They disappeared from the pages of history although it is believed that they subsequently found employment in the music business.

7. The remains of the Man Who Is Half Man And Half Biscuit formed the base of a tarte au citron which has been preserved and is on display in La Musee Des Beaux Biscuits in the village of Galettes d'Antan, Normandy (currently closed for refurbishment).[1]

8. *The Man Who Is Half Man And Half Biscuit — Fact or Fiction?* by AJP Blunt is currently out of print.

9. *A Brief History Of Biscuits* by Nigella Huntley and Kirsty Palmer is currently out of print.[2]

10. The Dangerous Hats Act (1887) was repealed in 1967.

Sub-Footnotes

1. In France the rights of gingerbread men are enshrined in *La Déclaration des droits des hommes de pain d'épice*, one of the founding documents of the French Revolution, written by M. Thomas Pain in 1789. In 1979, *La Société Nationale Pour L'Avancement Des Hommes De Pain D'Epice* was renamed *La Société Nationale Pour L'Avancement Des Hommes Et Femmes De Pain D'Epice*.

2. Doubt has been cast on Huntley and Palmer's credibility as serious historians due to their insistence in *Garibaldi - Man Or Biscuit?* that Italian general, politician and patriot Guiseppe Garibaldi was, in fact, a biscuit.

Sub-Sub-Footnote

1. *Garibaldi - Man Or Biscuit?* is currently out of print.

MINTBALL SQUARE

Mintball Square is probably best known today as the location of the long running Lancashire Radio soap opera *Mintball Square.*[1]

It is the former market square of Wigan but should have been more accurately called Mintball Dodecagon as it had twelve sides, no two of which were identical.

It is located at the intersection of a number of ley lines which criss-cross Lancashire.

Its bloodthirsty past includes public executions, a civil war battle and a mass brawl between supporters of Wigan RLFC and St Helens following a Rugby League Challenge Cup fourth round tie in 1923.[2]

It has been the scene of numerous mysterious and unexplained phenomena throughout the ages and is rated one of the most haunted places in Lancashire by *Which Ghost?* magazine and the local tourist board.[3]

Before the Industrial Revolution, it was a

Mintball Square: JJB Henshaw had the vision to make it the hub of a new Wigan

typical Lancashire village square with a church, an inn, a gift shop, a delicatessen and several estate agents.

Following the industrialisation of the town, they were replaced by a pound shop, a pawnbrokers, several takeaways, a bookies, a nail bar, a tanning salon and a tattoo parlour.

On 9 November 1852, an earthquake struck Wigan town centre which was felt as far away as Ashton-in-Makerfield and Billinge and caused over £30 worth of damage.[4]

The square was redeveloped by JJB Henshaw, a local businessman and philanthropist, who had emigrated to America with his wife in 1873. He made his fortune there having purchased the

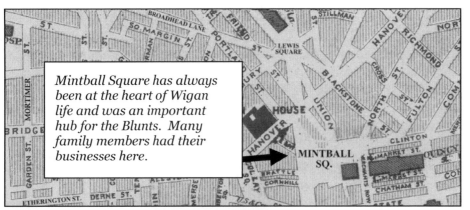

Mintball Square has always been at the heart of Wigan life and was an important hub for the Blunts. Many family members had their businesses here.

read about in Edinburgh.

Having spent time in the USA, however, Henshaw favoured a brasher style and the square emerged as a mixture of neo-classical, rococo and late baroque designs in something of an architectural mish-mash which was described by Prince Albert, in an editorial for *Gentleman's Architecture Monthly,* as 'an abcess, a cankerous pustule - a veritable cyst on the backside of Wigan'.[7]

Nevertheless, situated as it was close to the Leeds – Liverpool canal, the square not only benefited from the tourist trade but also became a popular place for the people of Wigan to shop and has played an important part in the town's history.

One notable event which occurred hereabouts was the Mintball Square Massacre of 1895. A policeman on a white horse charged into a crowd of a dozen people from the Competitive Movement demonstrating against government plans to reduce the amount of adulteration allowed in tea. In the confusion which ensued, four people were slightly injured. According to the *Wigan Courier and Argus,* a Mr Roy Rowlands of Birkdale was hit on the head with a truncheon whilst a Mr Rupert Murdstone, also of Birkdale, was hit in the face with a custard pie thrown

state of Florida from native Americans in exchange for two tins of shortbread, a Wigan RLFC supporters' club badge and his wife Nellie. He sold the land to a Russian billionaire the following year and returned to England where he later became the Mayor of Bamber Bridge.[5]

JJB Henshaw

Henshaw never forgot his roots and commissioned Charles Apple Macintosh, an apprentice architect of Scots origin, to draw up plans for the new look Mintball Square.[6]

Charles Apple Macintosh

When accepting the commission, Apple Macintosh had envisaged vistas of long, straight and wide boulevards lined by elegant houses similar to those he had

by a counter demonstrator from the Socialist Working Men's Party. Rowlands was charged with damaging police property and fined 2s.[8]

It remains a popular misconception that the square was named after the spherical sugar confection for which Wigan has achieved some minor notoriety but nothing could be further from the truth. Mintball

Count Johan Sebastian Minzeball

Square was originally called Minzeball Square and actually named after Count Johan Sebastian Minzeball of the House of Hapsburg, Imperial Vicar to the German Confederation, whom Henshaw had met whilst on holiday in Prussia and the Black Forest in 1899.

During the Great War, in a wave of anti-German sentiment, crowds gathered to demand the re-naming of the square to something more fittingly English. It was even considered that the square might be named after Uncle Bill's Meatballs but in the end the name was anglicised to Mintball Square.

In 1986, a fire in a fish and chip shop caused huge damage to one half of the square which was left largely derelict until most of Mintball Square was demolished in 1995 to make way for a handy multi-storey car park.[9]

Today, the car park is the main feature of Mintball Square. There is little sign of the square's bloodthirsty past but

Crowds gather in Minzeball Square, Wigan (1916) to demand the renaming of the Square.

strange goings on are still regularly reported. In 1947, the *Wigan & Ince Chronicle* reported that it 'rained cats and dogs' over the square for three consecutive days.

Mysterious sighs and groans can still be heard coming from the narrow alleys leading off the square, particularly after closing time on Friday and Saturday nights. Moreover, hundreds of cars have mysteriously disappeared from the car park.[10]

In 1999, Yvonne Fieldmouse, host of the popular cable TV programme *Most Frightening*, conducted an all night vigil in the car park. The sound of doors slamming and engines being ignited can be heard regularly throughout the programme but stop at 4am when the car park closes.

The Wigan Casino Bank opened in Mintball Square in November 1901 and by 1902 it had 32 branches around Wigan, seven of them in Mintball Square alone. [11]

The square also hosts the distinguished

St Martins College of Art, from which a succession of talented graduates has emerged and the Wigan School of Home Economics, from which a string of pies, pastries and cupcakes has emerged.

JJB Henshaw never forgot his roots and proved to be a great benefactor of the School, inaugurating the JJB Henshaw Chair of Politics, Philosophy and Shortbread in 1905, a seat which has since been held by many distinguished confectioners.[12]

Footnotes

1. The first episode was broadcast in 1923 and featured Pat Partridge as Elsie Stunner, Doris Gonzales as Annie Walters, William Spliff as Ken Marlow and Capt. Arthur Mainwaring as Albert Spatchcock.

2. Wigan won 28-26 thanks to a last minute try by Bickerstaffe.

3. In his book *Stranger Than Fact,* Graham Spatchcock refers to a local legend that the Holy Grail and the Ark of the Covenant are buried beneath the Church Of Zion in Mintball Square. In 2004, excavations led by Professor Tony Baldrick on the popular TV programme *Time Travellers* were abandoned after six weeks after only a child's shoe, a shopping trolley and several item of ladies undergarments were found.[1]

4. Approximately £18,800 at today's prices. This was a huge amount considering most of the shops were crude constructions. The church was destroyed but subsequently completely rebuilt. Only one building was left standing after the earthquake - 666 Mintball Square, a haberdashery owned by Mrs Lucy Fairclough. Mrs Fairclough was convicted of witchcraft at Wigan Assizes and was condemned to be burnt at the stake in the square. This sentence was subsequently commuted to a community service order when Judge Matthew Hopkinson was informed that the punishment of being burnt at the stake for witchcraft had been abolished two hundred years earlier.

5. In his biography of Henshaw, *The Mayor of Bamber Bridge*, Thomas Hartley writes that it was a special tin commemorating Queen Victoria's Silver Jubilee of 1862 which featured a picture of Hettie Flax, a well-known Queen Victoria look-alike and may now be worth more than the state of Florida, such is its rarity value.[2]

6. Macintosh was the great grandson of Angus Macintosh, an assistant quartermaster in Bonnie Prince Charlie's army who was in charge of the supply of waterproof clothing to the troops. When the army marched through Wigan on its way back to Scotland, Macintosh liked it so much he stayed.

7. Even the Bishop of Wigan was unimpressed, describing it in an article in *The Church Times* as 'a reet s**thole'.

8. The Mintball Square Massacre was the subject of the film musical *Mintballoo (1969)* with Marvin Lee as Rupert Murdstone and Jane Honda as Mrs Roy Rowlands.

9. In an article in *GHQ Magazine*, the Prince of Wales described the car park as 'a cyst, a cankerous abcess - a veritable pustule on the elbow of Wigan'. The Bishop of Wigan declined to comment.

10. This stopped when CCTV cameras were installed in 2004.

11. The business model whereby multiple branches of the same bank are opened on the same street was subsequently adopted by the Spanish-owned Santasdeer Bank in many parts of the UK.

12. The heyday of Mintball Square was in the Edwardian period when it attracted visitors from as far away as Ashton-in-Makerfield. At this time there were thriving haberdashers, fishmongers and tanning salons, as well as inns, taverns and fish pedicure stalls.[3]

Sub-Footnotes

1. The disruption caused by the excavations cost in excess of £200,000. The programme was never broadcast.

2. Hartley believes Henshaw bought Florida because he could see its potential as the location for an amusement park and holiday destination.

3. William Henry Blunt opened his first and only newsagents shop on Mintball Square, which also played host to Thomas Blunt & Sons travel agency between 1902 and 1995.

UNCLE BILL'S
MEAT-FREE MEATBALLS

In Lancashire today the name Blunt is synonymous with fridge magnets. There are few fridges which are not adorned with one of their fine hand-crafted products.

But it hasn't always been thus. There is another product which bears the name Blunt which briefly outshone the fridge magnets — Uncle Bill's Meat-Free Meatballs.[1]

Fast forward to 1918. Now back a bit. Stop. It's 1914 and Blunt's Mortimer Street Factory has been requisitioned by the War Office and dedicated to producing anti-German fridge magnets as part of the country's propaganda campaign.

Although it had been invented in 1913, the domestic refrigerator was still not affordable except for a few wealthy households and WG Blunt was becoming increasingly impatient. He now had more than 20,000 fridge magnet designs in his portfolio for the home market but no customers. He was struggling to make ends meet and finding it difficult paying his employees' wages.

The familiar red, white and blue roundel used to promote Uncle Bill's Meat-Free Meatballs. If you are reading the black and white version of this book, the blue roundel is in the middle.

Uncle Bill's Meatballs were the marketing sensation of 1916

'Uncle Bill' Blunt with Antonia (right) and family outside their Morecambe café (c.1917)

Not for the first time, he came up with the idea for a new business. But this time he had some success.

William's Uncle Bill was the younger brother of Isambard and was married to Antonia, the daughter of Italian soprano Basil Gnocchi. Together they ran *Antonia's Tripe and Pasta Hut,* an Italian café on Morecambe seafront.[2]

It served a fusion of the tastes of Lancashire and Italy such as fish, chips and pesto gravy, meat and potato lasagne and pizza with a reticular tripe topping.

The exotic marriage of the flavours of the Mediterranean and Irish Seas created a taste sensation and made even tripe palatable.

The café was popular with long-distance horse and carriage drivers, particularly those of mixed Lancashire and Italian descent. Dishes such as spaghetti wiganese, black pudding ice cream and sticky toffee tiramisu went down a treat.

But William's favourite dish was Antonia's meatballs. He wasn't the only one. Whenever he visited his uncle and aunt's café, he noticed that it was the meatballs which were by far the most popular dish.

He persuaded Aunt Antonia to give him her secret meatball recipe and paid government officials to let him supply the meatballs under licence to British troops, together with a free fridge magnet with each tin.

They were an instant hit. The soldiers couldn't get enough of the delicious dish and the fridge magnets came in useful for target practice.

Soldiers' wives back home in Lancashire knew that when the postman delivered an envelope with MRWIGH (Meatballs Ready When I Get Home) on the back,

40

that meant it was from their husbands.

One soldier even composed a marching song dedicated to the meatballs with the memorable chorus:

Stuff the bloomin' Germans
Stuff the bloomin' Gauls
All I want when I get home
Is Uncle Bill's Meatballs

The wartime poster that caught the spirit of the times

Encouraged by the positive response, William launched the meatballs on to the domestic market in 1916 backed up by a sophisticated advertising campaign by Charles and Maurice Spaatchcock featuring Uncle Bill in the style of Lord Kitchener. The rousing slogan *Get Some Balls* was perfect for a nation at war.

Then disaster struck. The war came to an end. This was bad news for William. Even worse, meat was to be rationed. There was some good news, though. Tripe was to be rationed, too and huge crowds came out on to the streets all over Lancashire to celebrate.

Knowing he had created an insatiable appetite for his meatballs, he decided to come up with a meat-free version. Uncle Bill's Meat-Free Meatballs were launched on to an unsuspecting public in

A huge crowd celebrates in Albert Square, Manchester on hearing the news that tripe is to be rationed

1918. Thanks to the tasty recipe with Italian herbs and a new advertising campaign by Spaatchcock and Spaatchcock which featured the world famous pacifist and vegetarian, Mahatma Gandhi, sales of Uncle Bill's Meat-Free Meatballs were just as high as they were for the original variety.[3]

The domestic refrigerator finally became widely available in the early twenties, though not many Lancashire folk could

Mahatma Gandhi with workers at William Blunt's meatball works during a visit in August 1929

afford to buy one. They were also suspicious of anything fancy and new-fangled and saw no reason why they shouldn't continue to store their milk, cheese, butter and other perishables in the outside toilet.

But William hardly noticed. He was too busy trying to meet the burgeoning demand for his tasty new meatball product to care about fridge magnets.

Then another disaster struck. In the early thirties, William decided he wanted to break into the lucrative German market which was dominated by *Dr Müller's Königsberger Klopse Ohne Fleisch*. On the advice of Spaatchcock and Spaatchcock, he decided to hire Adolf Hitler, an up and coming German politician, to promote his meat-free

When war broke out, the Hitler advertising posters were attacked by members of the public who defaced them with obscenities. His trademark fringe and moustache were removed with white paint.

meatballs in a new advertising campaign.

By 1936, it became clear that this had not been a wise decision. When war was declared, sales fell off a cliff — as did Uncle Bill shortly afterwards whilst walking Simon, his pet Yorkie, on Helvellyn on Christmas Day, 1939.

Footnotes

1. The meatballs should really have been branded Aunt Antonia's as they were based on her secret recipe. However, on Spaatchcock and Spaatchcock's advice they were called Uncle Bill's to capitalise on the patriotic fervour generated by the war and to protect against any anti-foreigner sentiment.

2. Aunt Antonia was briefly employed at the Wigan School of Home Economics as a visiting lecturer in Pasta Studies in the Department of Italian Gastronomy.

3. In 1929, Gandhi visited the factory to collect a free tin of Uncle Bill's Meat-Free Meatballs as a thank you when the millionth tin of Uncle Bill's Meat-Free Meatballs was sold.

4. Between 1915 and 1918, the huge presses at William Blunt and Son's Mortimer Street factory churned out

hundreds of thousands of anti-German fridge magnets. However, a world shortage of acrylic meant that they were simply stamped on to tin-plate and were therefore somewhat inferior in appearance. These magnets are now a rarity and can command as much as £3.50 on eBay.

The now rare anti-German fridge magnet produced by William Blunt & Sons between 1915 and 1918. Most were subsequently discarded, so surviving magnets have increased in value.

THE COMPETITIVE MOVEMENT

William Gladstone Blunt was greatly concerned by the spread across Europe of the twin spectres of socialism and egalitarianism.

Inspired by the work of Charles Marcus and Frederick Spangles, he decided to join a group of like-minded businessmen opposed to the exploitation of bosses by feckless workers who expected to be paid for their work. Some were even demanding a lunch break and an 80 hour working week.

Their first meeting took place in the cellar of Mr Michael O'Laoghaire's corner shop on Frog Lane in Birkdale, near Southport, on 7 October 1892.

It was attended by twenty-two businessmen from across the north including Cecil Sharp, a Yorkshire wool magnate, Rupert Murdstone, a publisher and Duncan Bannockburn, an ice cream salesman.

The meeting started at 6.30pm. At 6.45 they issued a declaration of the values and principles which would inform the way in which they would do business.

The Birkdale Trailblazers at their historic first meeting near Southport in 1892

Their values can be summed up as 'every man for himself' and 'from each according to his needs, to each according to his abilities'. There were no principles.

The group became known as The Birkdale Trailblazers (or Birks by their critics) and the movement they founded became known as The Competitive Movement.

They decided to pool their capital and launched a number of ventures including a money launderette in Salford, an insurance company and the world's first casino bank in Wigan.

Young people from all over Lancashire flocked to the Wigan Casino Bank to take out cheap loans and to participate in all night gambling sessions fuelled by the cheap booze which was made available to them.

The bank made huge profits by offering very high interest rates to savers and very low interest rates to borrowers. As soon as a new customer had been tied into a lengthy contract, it reversed its interest rates.

Its Competitive Insurance business charged premiums which seemed reasonable but refused to pay out when a customer made a claim.[1]

It would be unthinkable for such practices to exist today. But they became widespread and were codified in the bible of the Competitive Movement, Cecil Sharp's *Book Of Sharp Practices*.[2]

The Spaatchcock slogan that put The Comp at the forefront of the undertaking business

The Trailblazers pioneered the use of advertising to promote their businesses and paid pioneer admen Charles and Maurice Spaatchcock £25 — a huge sum

44

The first Comp Shop on Frog Lane, Birkdale — originally Mr Michael O'Laoghaire's, now a museum celebrating the movement's proud history

in those days — to come up with a slogan for its chain of funeral parlours.

For the shop in Birkdale, which sold everything from baby products to condiments and sauces, they came up with the slogan 'From Cradles To Gravy'.

The shop became the testing ground for many of the group's business theories.

O'Laoghaire's first move was to launch a range of own brand products, the first of which was 66 Tea. This proved to be a huge success because it was two-thirds the price of other teas. This was due to the fact that it contained 34% sawdust.

O'Laoghaire was a deep thinker and constantly exploring ways in which he could increase his profits. He introduced a 'no-frills' business model and removed all products with frills from his shop. A keen follower of the stock market, he noticed that the price of commodities would increase when they were scarce and fall when they were plentiful. So he decided to hide products in his cellar in

Comp '66' Tea was still popular as late as the 1970's

order to justify charging more for them in his shop.

When his profits began to fall because there were more goods in his cellar than in his shop, he offered unpaid work placements to teenagers to carry the goods back up to the shop and tried a different business model.

This time he hit upon the idea of appearing to charge much less than his competitors for his goods but to bill his customers for extras such as basket hire, issuing a receipt and leaving the shop.

He encouraged his customers to buy goods on credit at extortionate rates of interest and added a 10% service charge if the customer insisted on paying in cash. He refused to accept major credit cards, however, as they had not yet been invented.

By the time O'Laoghaire unlocked the doors and allowed his customers to leave the shop, their final bill would have doubled or tripled.[3]

Using the business practices espoused by The Birkdale Trailblazers, O'Laoghaire became a very wealthy man, growing his business from a single grocers into a chain of supermarkets which today has more shops than every other retailer put together and which is close to achieving

Duncan Bannockburn, aged 22

Duncan Bannockburn, aged 38 and his son, Hamish

Duncan Bannockburn, aged 62 and his dog, Hamish

its aim of having one store for every man woman and child in the country by 2020.

Sadly, The Birkdale Trailblazers didn't last long. At their second meeting, they disagreed about who should chair the meeting. Duncan Bannockburn declared himself out, chaos ensued and the local constabulary had to be called to restore order. Rupert Murdstone was rushed to the local infirmary with suspected

45

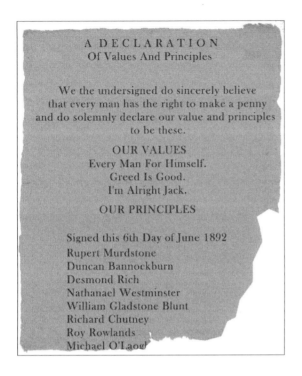

A DECLARATION
Of Values And Principles

We the undersigned do sincerely believe
that every man has the right to make a penny
and do solemnly declare our value and principles
to be these.

OUR VALUES
Every Man For Himself.
Greed Is Good.
I'm Alright Jack.

OUR PRINCIPLES

Signed this 6th Day of June 1892
Rupert Murdstone
Duncan Bannockburn
Desmond Rich
Nathanael Westminster
William Gladstone Blunt
Richard Chutney
Roy Rowlands
Michael O'Laogh

The original Competitive Charter and some of its 13 signatories. Nine of the original 22 attendees at the first meeting had stepped outside to settle a disagreement when the Charter was signed.

who dedicated their lives to creating wealth, particularly for themselves. With the benefit of hindsight, it is unsurprising that a movement of individuals fundamentally opposed to any form of collective action was clearly destined to fail.

All that remains of The Competitive Movement today is The Competitive Bank. But it can be safely said that The Competitive Movement has had a profound influence not only on British business but on such fine political thinkers as Baroness Spatchcock, Sir Rhodes Wackford-Blunt and Norman Hobbit.

It is 'The Comp' we have to thank for the state of the British high street today.

concussion but this turned out to be merely a bruised ego.

The Competitive Movement shattered into its component parts — individuals

---

Footnotes

1. Customers who wished to make a claim were referred to the small print in their contract.[1]

2. Mr Cecil Sharp was not present when the Charter was signed as he was involved in settling a disagreement with eight other attendees outside a nearby public house.[2]

3. The business model based upon charging for extra services has become popular in many businesses from UK airlines to massage parlours as far afield as Thailand.

Sub-Footnotes

1. The small print was invisible to the naked eye.[1]

2. The hospital records do not indicate the cause of the disagreement.

Sub-Sub-Footnote

1. This practice was subsequently outlawed by the Minimum Typesize Act (1921) which came into force following protests from compositors and printers.[*]

[*] The Minimum Typesize Act was repealed in 1983 following lobbying by ophthalmic opticians Messrs. Donald & Hutchison Ltd. trading as Specs-U-Like.

WIGAN CASINO BANK

Wigan Casino Bank was formed by the thirteen members of the Birkdale Trailblazers who had set up the Competitive Movement in 1892.

It functioned as a normal bank, charging huge interest on loans and paying hardly any interest on savings. To achieve a better rate of interest, customers could gamble their savings in the casino arm of the bank.

As the bank owned the gaming tables, it retained a percentage even when it paid out. This simple technique generated a fortune and, in its heyday the Wigan Casino Bank had seven branches in Mintball Square, Wigan, alone.

From the start, it proved to be a remarkable success, attracting capital from businesses across Wigan and the wider area. A robust series of takeovers and lucrative gambles paid off and, for a while at least, the bank was a rising star that gained the attention of investors as far afield as Billinge and Ashton-in-Makerfield.

Frederick Goodwin-Sands 1872 – 1903

The bank also pioneered the use of hole in the wall cash dispensers as early as 1898. The bank owners simply removed several bricks from an outside wall and issued customers with a uniquely numbered long stick or 'pin' which they could poke through the hole. A cashier inside the bank would recognise the 'pin' number and attach a ten shilling note.

Alas, the fortunes of the bank were to change in quite dramatic fashion when a new manager was appointed in 1902.

By all accounts a man of impeccable taste and habits, Frederick Goodwin-Sands gave no outward impression of dissolute ways. On Sundays he attended Methodist Chapel and was even observed purchasing flowers on Mothering Sunday in 1903.[1]

Yet this was nothing more than an elaborate façade. Goodwin-Sands was a secret, inveterate gambler and therefore the very last person you would want in charge of a Casino Bank.

Mr Maurice Balotelli (1868–1904): he exploded for one last time in 1903, causing the death of Frederick Goodwin-Sands. Mr Balotelli's family inherited 31 branches of the Wigan Casino Bank, reducing it to a shadow of its former self.

One night, in a rash move, he staked 31 of the company's 32 branches on a wager that he could go five rounds with Maurice Balotelli, The Exploding Man, a member of the Morocconi Brothers' Travelling Freak Show. After just one round, Balotelli exploded and Goodwin-Sands was blown to smithereens. The banks were lost and the company was reduced to the rump it is today.[2,3]

The sad death of Frederick Goodwin-Sands remains a salutary tale of the dangers of gambling and is a story told to children even today in the chapels and Sunday schools of Ashton-in-Makerfield,

Mintball Square, Wigan in 1902: branches of the Wigan Casino Bank compete for a customer

The distinctive logo of the Wigan Casino Bank. In 1962, the bank won the European Advertising Palm D'Or for their slogan: 'You Can Count On Us Just Under 50% Of The Time'.

Aspull and Billinge.

The Bank soldiered on through two world wars until it suddenly became popular in the 1960's when young people from all over Lancashire would flock there to take part in all night gambling sessions fuelled by copious supplies of cheap alcohol, mugs of tea and northern sole and chips supplied from Fleetwood.[4]

Footnotes

1. There is evidence to suggest that Mr Goodwin-Sands may have hired a look-alike to make this purchase as a way of providing a veneer of respectability for his gambling activities.

2. The collapse of the Wigan Casino Bank sent shock waves through the Lancashire banking system and led to government reforms separating casinos from banks 100 years later.

3. A government tax on adulterated tea led to the collapse of the bank in 1905 but it was bailed out and managed to continue in a much slimmed-down form.

4. In 2009, the bank was taken over by Große Metro Bank von Hannover (GMBH) GmbH as part of a major restructuring.

THE WIGAN SCHOOL OF HOME ECONOMICS

According to my observations, the average weight of a Lancashire man is around 11st whilst a Lancashire woman typically weighs in at 14st.[1]

The WSHE 's Faculty of Applied Domestic Science on Mintball Square

But things were very different at the turn of the century. Hard physical labour and a meagre diet consisting mainly of gruel and tripe meant that many men and women were not strong enough to do their jobs properly.

Motivated by a desire to improve the health of the working people of industrial Lancashire, the Wigan School of Home Economics was established in 1895 by Sidney and Beatrice Websyte and George Bernard Blunt. Using substantial government grant monies, their brief was to encourage the workers of Lancashire to adopt diets which would help them put on weight and become stronger. They instructed them in the preparation of pies, puddings and hotpot as well as more exotic fattening foods such as pasta and pizza — all on a budget of just 2d per person per week.

The School rapidly gained a reputation for developing recipes designed to tempt the palates of jaded workers all over the north west of England and for its radical political agenda.[2]

Delia Blunt, WSHE's first principal

Under the strict leadership of its principal Delia Blunt[3], the School recruited the finest French chefs and became known as the premier place for developing and perfecting recipes for dishes rich in calories. Mrs Blunt's synthesis of tripe and fine French cuisine was recognised when she was made an honorary member of *La Faculté de Préparation Tripes* at the Sorbonne School of Domestic Science in Paris.

In 1911, the WSHE moved from rooms at the rear of William Blunt and Sons' Mortimer Street factory to Mintball Square. The premises were officially opened by David George Lloyd on Bluntsday (7 October) 1911.[4]

During the Great War, the WSHE moved to a secret location where a crack team of domestic scientists worked to develop a recipe for the perfect cupcake which the government intended to lace with laxatives and drop in large quantities over the German trenches. This was kept a closely-guarded secret under the Government's Home Security (Cupcakes) Act of 1916.

When the Act was repealed in 2006, the release of the recipes led to an explosion in the production of cupcakes by small businesses. By January 2012, cupcake

The Blunt Recipe Magnet No 12: unique in being the only recipe in which the title is longer than the instructions

Beattie Norris fronted the WSHE 's adverts for pies in the 1950s

sales represented almost 15% of the UK's gross domestic product, with the industry employing more people than the NHS and the BBC put together. But it is the enduring popular association of Wigan with pies that is the real testimony to the School's continued success.[5,6]

Footnotes

1. Excluding tattoos.

2. The head of the home economics department for many years was Professor Prudehomme, a radical French chef who taught at the WSHE until his retirement in 1923.

3. Delia Blunt was a niece of William Gladstone Blunt and notable patron of Wigan RLFC.[1]

4. David George Lloyd was a David Lloyd George look-alike from Blackpool booked accidentally by the WSHE's office secretary. Her mistake only became apparent when, asked if he knew her father, he replied that he didn't.

5. In the 1930s, the School hired the Charles and Maurice Spaatchcock agency to pioneer the use of catchy advertising slogans to promote its pies. This continued with some success into the 1950s, as an advert featuring 'Grandma' Beattie Norris shows.[2] Wigan became

synonymous with pie-eating in the 1960s, when club comedian Bernard Manningham made eating three of them a staple part of his act.

6. In the period after the Second World War, the WSHE received substantial government funding to promote the idea that people should put on weight by eating '5-a-day': potatoes, pasta, ice cream, cheese, cake.

Sub-Footnotes

1. William Blunt and Sons' recipe fridge magnets were inspired by Delia Blunt's belief that with sufficient iron in their blood people could wear magnetic clothes. For his final eight years, WG Blunt lived only on boiled liver and cabbage in an attempt to increase the ferrous content of his blood to demonstrate its capacity to support magnetic clothing. Dieticians still debate whether a more varied diet would have extended or reduced this final eight years. One view is that had he increased the proportion of cabbage at the expense of liver, Blunt's visual acuity might have improved to such an extent that he would have seen the tram which killed him.

2. Beattie Norris later found fame when she was offered the role of Doris, the racist clippie, in the short-lived Granada TV series *Get Off My Bus* starring Reg Varnish.

SIDNEY & BEATRICE WEBSYTE

Sidney and Beatrice Websyte were radical socialists who were very influential in the establishment of the Wigan School of Home Economics using a bequest which had been left to the Fabio Society[1].

Sidney Websyte was born in 1859 and was from mining stock, one of the 'common people' fêted by the Fabios. He left school to work in the family mine at the age of 14, rising to become colliery manager within a few short weeks.

But his real interest was in making cakes and puddings and any spare time he had was spent baking in the family kitchen.

Whilst other miners were taking their snap of tripe butties to work, Sidney insisted on consuming elaborate baked cheesecakes, black forest gateaux or profiteroles.

Beatrice Potterswheel was born in 1858, the daughter of a wealthy industrialist who spurned her background to spend time with working class folk. She had grown up in Greece, had a thirst for knowledge and enrolled at St Martins

Sidney (left) and Beatrice (right) Websyte, founder members of the Wigan School of Home Economics. Her thirst for knowledge took her to St Martins College, where they met.

College in Wigan to study motor mechanics. According to her autobiography, that was where a young Sidney Websyte caught her eye. She reputedly told him that her Dad was loaded and he said in that case he would have a rum and coca-cola.

They later went to a supermarket and discussed renting a flat above a shop and getting Beatrice's hair re-styled. She records in her diary how they then bought some cigarettes and visited a pool hall.[2]

After marrying, the Websytes threw their energies into establishing the Wigan School of Home Economics. In 1912, Sidney became Honorary Professor in the Faculty of Baked Confectionery, overseeing the development of a series of cupcake recipes which were later appropriated by the government for use in both world wars. [3]

Along with George Bernard Blunt, the Websytes became supporters of the Soviet Union when it was established in 1917. They regularly visited Russia and their books, *Soviet Communism: A New Land of Marxist Home Economics (1935)*[4] and *The Truth About Soviet Kitchens (1936)*[5] show Joseph Stalin's regime in a very positive light.

The Stalin-Hitler Pact of 1939 threw the Websytes into disarray. A schism had been developing at the Wigan School of Home Economics and uncertainties about the future direction of communism widened it. One element led by Mr Everard Kipling splintered off to form the College of Marxist Home Economics in Billinge while the more liberal members remained in Wigan.[6,7]

The Websytes died in mysterious circumstances in 1939[8] but their legacy to domestic science — and in particular the development of the cupcake — lives on to this day.

Soviet Communism: the Websytes wrote extensively of their trips to Russia in the early 1930's

---

Footnotes

1. The Society was established by Fabio Llewellyn-Bowen, a hairdresser from Blackburn.

2. A series of misprints in AJP Blunt's biography of the Websytes, *Common People*, caused the first edition to be pulped.

3. The noted patriotic poet and baker Mr Rudyard Custard-Crème was briefly Emeritus Professor of Politics, Philosophy and Choux Pastry at the WSHE.

4. *Soviet Communism: A New Land of Marxist Home Economics* is currently out of print.

5. *The Truth About Soviet Kitchens* is currently out of print.

6. Kipling was described by his colleagues as an 'exceedingly good' vice-chancellor of the Billinge College.

7. In the 1970s, militant *meringuistas* from the Billinge campus were found to have enrolled surreptitiously on to courses at Wigan. They were accused of 'entryism' and expelled.

8. Sidney and Beatrice were killed in a freak accident when their separate gliders collided over a remote part of Lancashire in late 1939. Until their death neither had shown any interest in gliding and there is some suspicion that they were killed by agents of the NKVD cake division working from a kitchen in Chorley, Lancashire.

ST MARTINS COLLEGE OF ART & MECHANICAL ENGINEERING

St Martins College of Arts and Mechanical Engineering is widely regarded by its alumni as one of the leading art and mechanical engineering institutions in Wigan.[1,2,3]

St Martins School of Tropical Medicine and Fine Art, Mintball Square, Wigan

The College was formed in 1989 from the merger of the Wigan School of Civil Engineering and Dance, founded in 1856 and St Martins School of Tropical Medicine and Fine Art, founded in 1854.[4]

The latter institution produced some of the most elaborate — and highly sought after — medicine packaging the north west has ever seen, although the contents often proved to be highly toxic. In 1873, there was a public outcry following the poisoning of three colliery banksmen in Parbold and the deputy principal, Dr David Livingstone was convicted of gross negligence and serious medical malpractice.

Students from the School of Civil Engineering and Dance have been involved in the design of a number of landmark buildings across the north west including the Knott End Tower and

Ballroom, the Runcorn Bridge and Dance Hall, the sprung floor of the Birkenhead Tunnel Palais and the M66 Dance Pavilion near Bury.

Isambard Kingdom Blunt was briefly a visiting lecturer at the college and it has played a significant role in the history of Wigan, extending its

Knott End Tower and Ballroom

influence to satellite colleges in Billinge and Ashton-in-Makerfield.

Located on the south side of Mintball Square, the School escaped the bulldozer when much of the rest of the square was demolished following a major fire in the

53

1980s. Luminaries of St Martins include:

Adrian Anthony Pint (b 1954) - a British writer who uses the byline A.A. Pint. He is currently employed by *The Wigan Argus & Parbold Chronicle* as their restaurant reviewer and motoring critic. His published essays have often caused offence to various groups, including the entire county of Yorkshire and drivers of Renault cars.

Gilbert Proust (b 1943) and **George Passport** (b 1942) - two artists who work together as a duo called **Proust & Passport** and who have been criticised for the inclusion of shocking imagery in their work, including nudity and fridge magnets. Works such as *Naked Fridge Magnet Pictures* (1994) caused particular offence.

Spike Leigh (b 1943) - a British writer and director of TV adverts with advertising agency Spaatchcock and Spaatchcock who pioneered gritty 'kitchen sink realism' advertising. His controversial, foul-mouthed ad for washing up liquid was withdrawn after just two airings. He found success as

Mike Hardy

director of feature films such as *Mintballs are Sweets* (1990) and *Meatballs and Pies* (1996).[5]

Mike Hardy (b 1944) - a former builder who began performing as a comedian at Workingmen's Clubs across the north west. When audiences failed to be amused by his comedy, he began introducing musical interludes into his act and in time they became the main focus of his act. He was known colloquially as 'The Wigan Cowboy' principally for the quality of his building work.

Jarvis Blunt (b 1963) - a shaven-haired exponent of the ChavPop musical genre and the lead singer of the Aspull-based rock and pop group, *Pap*. In 1988, Blunt took a sabbatical from the band to study Fine Art and Polymer Engineering at St Martins, where he graduated in 1991. He was arrested after over-exuberant Bluntsday celebrations in Wigan in October 1993.

Footnotes

1. St Martins achieved university status in 2009.

2. The University was the first in the country to offer a degree in Advanced Meatball Studies. The course is now also taught at the Universities of Penrith, Uttoxeter and Daventry.

3. Barbara Blunt, daughter of Bill Blunt, the current chief executive of William Blunt & Sons, graduated in Applied Makeup and Hair Removal in 1991 and undertook postgraduate studies in Nail Engineering for

a further five years. She never actually completed her MSc.

4. The Wigan School of Civil Engineering and Dance was formed in 1856 by the merger of the West Wigan School of Fine Art and Engineering and the East Wigan College of Dance and Fabric Conditioning.

5. *Meatballs and Pies* won the *Golden Shot Award* for best film at the St Annes Film Festival in 1996.

THE CAPITALISTS' EDUCATION ASSOCIATION, CHARLES MARCUS & FREDERICK SPANGLES

The success of William Blunt & Sons is owed in no small part to the visionary work of three men: Albert Porridge of Oldham, Frederick Spangles of Salford and Charles Marcus of Wigan.

It was Porridge who set up the first branch of the Capitalists' Education Association (CEA) and it was at the St Helens branch of the CEA that William Gladstone Blunt finally learned how to master business success.

Without the CEA, there may never have been a Competitive Movement and the Sharp Business Practices for which capitalism is renowned may well have stayed confined to the fringes of Yorkshire and the mind of Mr Cecil Sharp.

Porridge's story has already been ably told by AJP Blunt and permission has been obtained to include an extract from his pamphlet, which is reprinted on page 58. But few know of the role played by Marcus and Spangles in the development of the CEA.

The book that changed the course of business practice in many parts of Lancashire

Frederick Spangles was the son of Harriet and Boris Spangles, a wealthy German family of sweet manufacturers who sent him to work at their factory in Salford to find out why it was losing so much money.

He put on a false beard and went undercover using the pretext that he was the owner's son and wanted to find out why the factory was losing so much money.

None of the workers had ever travelled outside Salford nor had they heard a thick German accent before so they believed him when he told them that he was from Burnley and that was how they spoke there.

55

Frederick Spangles

He was appalled by what he found on the shop floor. The workers were organising into trades unions, taking time off and smuggling sweets out of the factory.

He dealt with the workforce ruthlessly, sacking anyone over the age of nine and increasing the hours and cutting the pay of those who remained. He also gave himself a huge pay rise via shares in a bogus off-shore company.

He then proceeded to revamp the product range, introducing a healthier range of sweets which were boiled rather than deep fried and which contained natural ingredients - milk bottles which contained real milk, porky pigs which contained real pork and acid drops which contained real sulphuric acid.

He also increased their sugar content and signed a sponsorship deal with local dentists which made him very wealthy indeed.

The Story of Marcus & Spangles

Marcus and Spangles met on Wigan Market where Marcus had a stall on which everything cost one halfpenny.

It was the most popular stall on the market. People would travel for miles to shop there — particularly people from Birkenhead who could buy products which cost £1 back home for just a halfpenny.

He didn't just sell the usual tat. You could pick up anything for a halfpenny from alabaster figurines, designer shawls and clogs to diamond rings, expensive timepieces and heavy machinery. The vast range of goods would change regularly. You could even order goods which he didn't have in stock.

Spangles couldn't work out how Marcus managed to sell such expensive goods so cheaply but recognised him as a man cut from the same cloth. He began supplying Marcus with his sweets, displayed in a pick'n'mix section which became popular with customers and soon they decided to go into business together. They opened their first shop which quickly became a chain of Marcus and Spangles' Halfpenny Bazaars, which was sold in 1906 for a huge sum to FW Duckworth.[1]

They founded the Wigan branch of the Capitalists' Education Association the following year and wrote *The Capitalist Manifesto* with its famous opening line, 'Bosses of the world unite. You have nothing to lose but your chain stores.'[2]

Charles Marcus

Charles Marcus had been a student of politics, philosophy and home economics under old Professor Prudehomme, a radical French chef at the Wigan School of Home Economics, and had spent hours poring over the works of Thomas Brighthouse, David Ocado and Mrs Beeton in the marble reading room of the huge municipal library in Mintball Square.[3]

One day, as he was pondering the theory of surplus value, he hit upon the formula $x > y = £££$ where x equals the price at which a product is sold and y equals the price at which it is bought. He suddenly realised that, if he could sell goods for more than he paid for them, he would make a profit. It therefore followed that the less he paid for his goods and the more he sold them for, the bigger the profit would be.

"Philosophers have merely interpreted the world," he thought to himself, "the point is to make money." So to put his theory to the test, he took a stall on Wigan Market selling second hand doors. But business was slow. It didn't take him long to realise that most people couldn't afford to buy a door as they didn't have two brass farthings to rub together. He would have to sell goods which were affordable and source them as cheaply as possible.

He remembered his old tutor, Professor Prudehomme, telling him all property is theft. If that was so, Marcus thought, he was perfectly entitled to steal other people's goods as they were not legally theirs. This was the light-bulb moment which set him on the road to riches.

Footnotes

1. Duckworths continued to sell goods for a halfpenny until they finally went bankrupt with massive debts in 1969 when the halfpenny ceased to be legal tender.

2. Marcus and Spangles went on to write many other books including *The Condition of the Middle Class in England* and *The Theory of Buy One Get One Free*. All are currently out of print.

3. The Wigan School of Home Economics was a hotbed of radical home economics at this time. Prudehomme was a champion of the anarchist school which opposed the use of recipes and favoured the use of any ingredients which came to hand. He was firmly opposed to the more authoritarian Marxist school, according to which recipes had to be followed to the letter and ingredients were strictly controlled. Recipes were often planned as long as 5 years in advance. [1]

Sub-Footnote

1. In December 1912, Prudehomme was arrested on his way home from college carrying a suspicious parcel following a number of explosions in Mintball Square but was released when police discovered nothing more sinister than a double chocolate bombe torte he had prepared for Christmas. It was later discovered that the explosions had been caused by gas leaks.

THE PARTNERSHIP BETWEEN CAPITAL AND LEARNING

The founder of the Capitalists' Education Association was a man who had left school at the age of fourteen and joined the family firm in Oldham as vice-chairman. Through sheer ineptitude in business matters, he ruined the company and ended his life as an office boy.

At the age of 57, Albert Porridge, vowed to learn from his mistakes and enrolled on a correspondence course in business practice run by John Stuart Miliband. In this way, he became very involved in the educational work of the Competitive Movement. However, his learning convinced him that there was a gap in the market for a place where men of capital could meet and learn the basics of ensuring that their businesses could thrive.

Albert Porridge (back, far left) at the first class of the Capitalists' Education Association in Oldham, 1890.

Being a man of some action as well as a true visionary, Porridge took the first step towards founding such an association - though it was Mrs Porridge who became the first member. She handed him 2s. 6d. from her housekeeping money as the first member's fee and together they elected themselves honorary secretary and founder member of the 'Association to Promote the Higher Education of Men of Capital'. The new Association was formally created at a conference in 1891 of Mr and Mrs Porridge and their representatives. Two years later, the Association rebranded itself as the Capitalists' Educational Association before settling in 1894 on the more familiar Capitalists' Education Association, at which point women were banned from membership.

Extract from *From Boardroom to Tea Boy: The History of the CEA* by AJP Blunt, 1949 (currently out of print). *Reprinted with kind permission of Murdstone Press.*

It's the drink Lancastrians enjoy first thing in the morning and last thing at night and as often as possible in between. Beer.

But few Lancastrians would disagree that there is nothing better than a nice cup of tea and a cupcake. For many people, the tea break is probably the most enjoyable part of the working day. In many workplaces it can last for up to an hour rather than the permitted fifteen minutes, especially when there are no supervisors or managers present. The latest government figures suggest that a typical Lancastrian consumes over 100 cups of tea a day, falling to four cups if council workers are excluded.

Tea was first brought to Lancashire by Chinese immigrants on their way to build the railroads in America. The inventive and enterprising people of Lancashire soon discovered the versatility of the tea plant and used every part of it to make a range of products such as tea shirts, tea bags and tea towels, which are still popular to this day.

But it was the delicious beverage made from the leaves of the tea plant which proved the most popular product and it

Model smugglers at the popular Teaworld theme park near Chorley

quickly became the favourite drink of Lancashire folk. Apart from beer. But for the ordinary working man, it was also very expensive because of the high taxes levied by the government and a black market in smuggled tea soon developed.

The tea arrived by rowing boat at towns such as Blackpool and Lytham St Annes. These Fylde towns were the main ports of entry on account of the large number of elderly people living there who had acquired a taste for tea and needed regular supplies to feed their habit.[2] The smugglers, exhausted from having rowed thousands of miles from China, would hand their tea chests over to 'middlemen' who would load them on to mules. The so called 'tea mules' were the main means by which the tea was distributed throughout Lancashire.

The tea would end up on the streets of the county's industrial towns or in corner shops and would often be adulterated by unscrupulous shopkeepers to boost their profits. The adulterated tea became known as 'fools tea' to distinguish it from unadulterated or 'proper tea'.[3]

When this came to the attention of the government, it drafted legislation to limit the extent to which dealers could adulterate their tea. Under the proposed legislation, fools tea had to be at least 10% tea. Shopkeepers saw this as an attack on their rights and, inspired by the writings of Marcus and Spangles, they launched a campaign to resist the new legislation under the banner 'Make Proper Tea History'.

In the long, hot summer of 1895, protests were held against the proposed legislation throughout the county. In Tottington near Bury, angry shopkeepers rioted, destroying the hanging baskets which decorated many people's houses, while a demonstration in Wigan ended in four protesters being slightly hurt. In Bolton, shopkeepers dumped chests of tea into the River Croal in what became known as The Bolton Tea Party.

The crackdown on smuggling led to a fall in supply and a huge increase in proper tea prices. When ordinary folk could no longer afford it, the banks began offering cheap loans to help people purchase their favourite tipple. The price of proper tea continued to rise almost daily and the loans got bigger and cheaper. Many people no longer regarded tea as a refreshing beverage but saw it as an investment. They bought more than they needed and hoarded it, confident it would continue to increase in price. The main talking point in the mills, mines and look-alike agencies of Lancashire was proper tea prices. Many people took out loans against their proper tea to pay for luxuries such as a front door, a holiday in Blackpool or a new horse and cart.[4]

Tea became so valuable that there was a huge increase in tea-related crime. Corner shops were raided, burglaries increased and the Royal Bank of Lancashire built new vaults to store its vast tea deposits.

In 1905, the government decided that the only way to stop the crime wave was to cut the taxes it levied on tea. Overnight, the price of tea fell, signalling the end of the proper tea boom, tea smuggling and the collapse of the Wigan Casino Bank.

Footnotes

1. For centuries, Lancashire has welcomed immigrants attracted by its climate, first rate transport links and proximity to Cheshire. The first Jews settled in Salford in biblical times whilst it is thought that the first curry house opened in Blackburn in the fifteenth century. It is not widely known that the source of the River Irwell was discovered by an African.

2. All day tea dances were extremely popular with older folk and would often go on until 10pm.

3. Fools tea would often be 'spiked' with chamomile, nettle or peppermint. It is thought that tea spiked with coca leaves and other hallucinogens was served at all night tea dances at Wigan Casino Bank.

4. At the height of the boom, the Wigan Casino Bank was paying customers to take out loans and many people's homes were so full of tea chests that they had to live in just one room.

THE BADEN-POWELL LOOK-ALIKE AGENCY

Even the most cursory of internet searches will confirm that today there are many hundreds of thousands of people employed by look-alike agencies up and down the country who are making a very good living indeed by looking nothing like the celebrities they are supposed to resemble.

The Baden-Powell twins from Birkenhead launched the first Look-Alike agency in Britain

It is widely believed that the look-alike agency is a modern phenomenon. But nothing could be further from the truth. The first look-alike agency was established by the Baden-Powell twins in Birkenhead in 1856.

The demand for look-alikes was fuelled by wealthy and powerful individuals who wanted to be in more than one place at the same time. So, for example, rather than fulfilling an official engagement such as opening a new mill or branch of the Wigan Casino Bank, a wealthy but indolent person could be at home playing croquet or perhaps taking tea with one of his mistresses.

Alternatively, for the more industrious individual for whom there simply weren't enough hours in the day, employing the services of a competent look-alike could help them to get more done.

There is now evidence to suggest that Sir Francis Drake had a look-alike who sailed in an exact replica of *The Golden Hind* to help him complete his epic circumnavigation of the globe in record time, whilst Witchfinder General Matthew Hopkins is said to have employed at least five look-alikes to enable him to conduct trials and execute witches at a much faster rate.

But being a look-alike wasn't all fun. It could be a very dangerous occupation indeed. Look-alikes were often employed

61

by political or military leaders and placed in dangerous situations or sent to the battlefield. In his book, *The Book of Nineteenth Century Look-Alikes*, AJP Blunt expounds the theory that there were as many as six Napoleons and three Dukes Of Wellington on the field of battle at Waterloo at any one time.[1]

Lord Nelson's look-alike, a Wigan blacksmith called John Wragg, had to have an eye and an arm removed after the Battles of Calvi and Santa Cruz respectively in order to maintain a close physical resemblance to his seafaring double. Unfortunately, surgeons removed the wrong arm and Wragg had to be replaced by another look-alike.

A strong physical resemblance wasn't always enough to maintain the deceit. One of the most successful look-alikes in history was George Frederick King, a Litherland costermonger, who bore a quite uncanny resemblance to King George IV.

George King, a costermonger from Liverpool, made a handsome living from his public appearances

King George was frequently indisposed due to his extravagant lifestyle and George King was often called upon to fulfil his official duties. After 40 years in the role, he was finally exposed in 1826 when, under the influence of alcohol, he declared Parliament open in a thick Scouse accent.

The existence of look-alikes has led to conspiracy theories such as David Spike's view that Hitler did not die in 1945 but was still alive and working as a window cleaner in Preston until 1972.[3]

Being a look-alike could be a lucrative line of work and could lead to fame and fortune for those at the top of their profession like the Baden-Powells.

Edward Baden-Powell famously said he knew he had become successful when look-alikes of him began to advertise their services. In fact, one look-alike became so wealthy that the person he was hired to be a look-alike for ended up as his look-alike. But for those who had the misfortune not to resemble a wealthy or eminent individual, it was a tough and often unrewarding occupation.

Jabez Cowell was the proprietor of by far the most down-market agency on the Wirral at that time which styled itself as a 'looky-likey' agency to appeal to popular tastes.

Jocelyn Jessop, a Sidney Websyte looky-likey and winner of 1898 Specs Factor competition. He was stripped of the title when it was revealed he had been wearing pince-nez at the time.

The agency was a major sponsor of local talent competitions such as *The Specs Factor* in which spectacle-wearing looky-likeys had to parade themselves in front of audiences whilst performing musical numbers at Birkenhead's Argyle Street Theatre.[4]

Probably the most notorious look-alike agent of the time was Malachi McClaren who was the mastermind behind the so-called 'Fake Silver' Jubilee celebration of 1862.

McClaren decided to earn some publicity for his agency by hiring a boat and sailing down the River Mersey to mark Queen Victoria's Silver Jubilee. The boat set off from Woodside in Birkenhead bound for the Pier Head, Liverpool via New Brighton on Saturday, 28 June at around 2pm.

Crowds gather to watch the 'Fake Silver' Jubilee flotilla

On board with McClaren were many of the celebrity look-alikes on his books including Benjamin Disraeli, Florence Nightingale and the royal couple, Queen Victoria and Prince Albert, as well as The Birkenhead Male Voice Choir.

It was a warm Saturday afternoon and many people were out strolling along the waterfront. When the choir started to sing God Save The Queen, crowds began

Alfred Tennyson (left) and his looky-likey George Sprague (right)

to gather and vessels started to follow the boat, creating a small flotilla.

Suspicions were aroused when an alert member of the public remembered that Prince Albert had unfortunately died the previous year. He summoned the river constabulary who set off in pursuit of the boat and successfully boarded it as it approached New Brighton.

When they attempted to arrest the Queen Victoria look-alike, she swore blind she was the real monarch so they attempted to arrest the look-alike consort as they knew the real Prince Albert to be dead.

He resisted arrest and a scuffle ensued. The poet laureate Alfred Tennyson look-alike took a swing at the arresting officer and succeeded in knocking him overboard.

Tennyson was taken into custody and charged with impersonating a poet and assaulting a police officer. He was found guilty and sentenced to ten years hard labour but received a royal pardon when it emerged that he was the real Alfred Tennyson and was standing in for his look-alike who was busy doing a book signing on his behalf at the Liverpool branch of Wilderspools.

The whole episode was recorded in meticulous detail in Tennyson's diaries for June 1862 and made the front page of that week's *Birkenhead Beagle*.

One of the most popular look-alikes in Birkenhead was Mr Harold Cholmondley who successfully impersonated US President Abraham Lincoln, largely because few people knew what Lincoln actually looked like. He dined out on his resemblance to Lincoln but his career came to an abrupt end in 1864.

The assassination of Harold Cholmondley by John Booth Wilkes at the Argyle Street Theatre, Birkenhead

He was visiting the theatre in Birkenhead with fellow look-alikes Hettie Flax (Queen Victoria) and Georgina Phelps (Florence Nightingale) when he was assassinated by a Mr John Booth Wilkes (a John Wilkes Booth look-alike who was visiting Birkenhead). The assassin escaped and fled to America.

In the 1920s, Wilfred Moss, a Stockport chimney sweep and Mahatma Gandhi look-alike, was fortunate enough to earn a lucrative sponsorship deal to be the face of Uncle Bill's Meat-Free Meatballs. But there was a far more sinister side to the world of look-alikes.

An honourable profession was given a bad name by a number of unscrupulous individuals who sought to benefit from their resemblance to others by committing crimes and passing themselves off as their look-alikes.

As a consequence, many upstanding and

Wilfred Moss from Stockport made a fortune in the 1920s as a Gandhi look-alike

virtuous members of the community had their reputations damaged and were punished for crimes they did not commit.[5]

Hettie Flax, perhaps the best known Queen Victoria look-alike of her generation, was also a notorious pickpocket who amassed a small fortune and only managed to escape punishment by invoking royal privilege.

In 1853, the Bishop of Wigan was forced to resign after being found guilty of head-butting a police constable one Saturday night in Mintball Square, Wigan, whilst drunk and disorderly. The crime had actually been committed by Duncan Bannockburn, an ice-cream salesman and part-time Bishop of Wigan look-alike. The Bishop did not have an alibi, was fined 10s and forced to resign.

Duncan Bannockburn and his dog Hamish: his resemblance to the Bishop of Wigan allowed him to embark on an undetected three month crime spree

The following year, Josiah Sharples, a petty criminal and David Livingstone lookalike, committed all manner of heinous crimes before being convicted for the theft of his next door neighbour's donkey. It was only when Livingstone returned to Britain from his African

How the Wigan Globe & Argus broke the story of David Livingstone's imprisonment

Within the newspaper clipping:

...sad experience he ha... therefore launched a Parliamentary petition with the aim of securing a new law making it an offence to sound a bell after the hours of 8 o'clock in the evening and to prohibit the slamming of carriage doors outside of public houses and hostelries.

FAMOUS SCOTTISH EXPLORER JAILED

Mr. David Livingstone, the well known Scottish explorer, is languishing in Wigan jail after being convicted of the theft of his neighbour's donkey. Mr. Livingstone, 42, of Gasworks Street, Hindley, was sentenced to ten years hard labour after admitting to the theft of Daisy, a four year old donkey belonging to his next door neighbour Mr. Alfred Sweet.

MORE COAL FOUND

A new seam of coal has been discovered near Wigan, making the total number of seams hereabouts a round 40. Mr. Ephraim Farraby has...

YET A... BRID... FAIL...

Reports hav... office of the col... another bridge... apprentice eng... Isambard Kingdom B...

The small bridge sp... River Tawd at... collapsed at appro... o'clock in the... Saturday last, a... injury to Mr. Edw... and his horse, w... the swirling waters...

According to Mr Co... was carrying a la... gold dust and seve... diamonds about his... and these were quite... the water. He is to... claim against Mr... through the fir... WeSueAnyOne & So... Bolton, who are a... specialist of some no...

This is the third... collapse in as many... these parts, and it... that questions are to b... about the competence... Blunt and his engin... firm. If you believe yo... suffered a grievance... the actions of this ma... are invited to contac... George Gussetton...

Josiah Sharples

expedition that the deception was revealed and his name was cleared.[6]

The most notorious gang of look-alikes were the Wanderers, a fraternity of petty

Albert Jessop of the 11-strong Wanderers, petty criminals who plied their trade on the football field

criminals and former shipyard workers from Liverpool who were the look-alikes of the Bolton Wanderers football team.

In 1894, first division Bolton were hot favourites to beat second division Notts County at Goodison Park to win the FA Cup for the first time in their history.

The gang placed a huge bet on County to win the match at odds of 20/1, kidnapped the Bolton team at their Warrington hotel the night before the final and locked

The Wanderers settled in the Basque area of Spain, where they went on to work in the region's shipyards

them in the cellar of The Dog and Bone public house, Widnes.

The gang played the final and lost 4-1 to Notts County with a late consolation goal scored by a look-alike of Jim Cassidy, the Bolton Wanderers centre forward.

Footnotes

1. *The Book of Nineteenth Century Look-Alikes* is currently out of print. A photocopy of the book is available on request from the Oxton Reference Library, Wirral (currently closed for refurbishment).

2. The Jabez Cowell Agency developed a reputation for 'low-rent' looky-likeys. In 1898 they were exposed as using two men—William and Frederick Fellows—dressed in women's clothing to pose as Florence Nightingale and her sister for the opening of a local cottage hospital in Hoylake. It brought to an end their 15 year career as the Nightingale Sisters.

3. Phenomenologist Graham Spatchcock has claimed that David Spike was actually the incarnation of a celestial visitor to planet Earth.

4. In 1861, John and Edward Baden-Powell entered the competition as look-alikes of themselves. They came fourth.

5. In 1876, The League for the Protection of Innocent Look-Alikes estimated that there were more than 400 men, women and children languishing in Lancashire jails for crimes perpetrated by criminal look-alikes.

6. Conspiracy theorist David Spike believes it was the real Livingstone who stole the donkey and that the source of the Nile was discovered by Josiah Sharples.

The Nightingale Sisters

JAMES BLUNT & BLUNTSDAY

James Blunt was the author of *Achilles*, the classic modernist novel in which the Trojan War is transposed, updated and condensed into a Friday night out in Wigan.

It was banned for many years due to its graphic accounts of sex and violence but mainly because much of it is written in classical Greek and in a style which Blunt called 'river of consciousness' (an extension of stream of consciousness but with no spaces between the words), rendering the book incomprehensible to all but scholars of classical Greek.

Blunt met his future wife, the formidable Yootha Barnstaple, whilst he was a student at the North Wigan College of Literature and Aeronautical Design and she was working down the pit.

Yootha had won the Lancashire's Strongest Woman competition four years running and was a very useful bare knuckle boxer, having won the silver medal at the 1918 Lancashire Games when she defeated Ethel Clegg by a knockout after a gruelling contest which lasted two days.[1]

Achilles: an orgy of sex, vomiting and pies

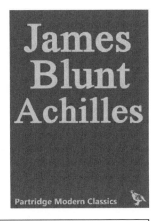

An extract from Achilles: in a scathing review in 1922, the literary editor of the Aspull News called it 'unreadable'

He bumped into her as he was cycling across one of the many bridges over the Leeds-Liverpool canal on his way to class and fell off his bike. Infuriated, she picked him up and threw him off the bridge into the canal.[2]

Blunt was clearly captivated by this powerful woman and they married shortly afterwards.[3] They led a peripatetic life moving from one town to another but he never forgot his birthplace and wrote *Achilles* as a tribute to it.

Yootha Barnstaple

Bluntsday is celebrated on 7 October every year to commemorate the day on which Blunt and Barnstaple met.[4] Originally, there was a range of cultural activities including readings from *Achilles*, dramatisations of scenes from the book and talks by visiting academics.[5] Hardcore devotees of the book once held marathon readings of the entire novel, some lasting up to two weeks.

Sadly, the origins of Bluntsday have been forgotten and all that remains today are pitched battles between rival gangs of 'Greeks' and 'Trojans' and re-enactments of the historic meeting of James Blunt and Yootha Barnstaple when young women toss young men off bridges into the canal.

James & Yootha Blunt

Bluntsday celebrations in Wigan, 2007: an orgy of sex, vomiting and colliery bands

---

Footnotes

1. Ethel Clegg retired from boxing and went on to find minor fame as a bit-part actress in the Spatchcock studios in Hollinwood. Her final role was as a waitress appearing alongside George Fleetwood in *Turned Out Ince Again* in 1941.

2. Blunt wrote in his diary for that day, 'I bumped into her as I was cycling across one of the many bridges over the Leeds-Liverpool canal on my way to class and fell off my bike. Infuriated, she picked me up and tossed me off'.

3. Although Blunt was besotted by Barnstaple, it is by no means clear that his feelings were reciprocated. The young Yootha had also caught the eye of one Arthur Joseph Mamby, a poet, barrister and civil servant who was also a talented amateur photographer and a Fellow of the Lancashire Society of Arts. Barnstaple's diaries show that she modelled for Mamby on a number of occasions (including after she had left her job at the pit when Mamby persuaded her to 'black up' again 'for old time's sake'). Mamby eventually became jaded by Wigan

collier women and moved to a semi by the sea in Fleetwood where he photographed local fisherwomen, leaving a heartbroken Yootha in Wigan to pick up the pieces.

4. Graham Spatchcock has speculated that Bluntsday may have assimilated an ancient Lancashire holiday called 'Firsday', originally a Druid festival held every week between Wednesday and Friday in the Forest of Bowland, on which a young fir tree had its needles ripped off before being sacrificially burnt by the High Priest. Over time, local people became confused about when exactly the holiday was held and it fell into disuse until it was picked up by the Wigan Tourist Board and standardised as 7 October in an attempt to popularise connections between the town and James Blunt.

5. *Achilles* tells the story of the rivalry between Achilles Warburton and Hector Grimshaw for the affections of the beautiful Helen Arkwright, 'the face that launched a thousand narrow boats'. It is currently out of print.

GEORGE IRWELL

Eric Arthur Blunt was born in Wigan in 1903. He lived with his parents and twelve siblings in a room above Walter Spiegelman's photographic studio in Mintball Square.

Eric described his family as 'lower working class'. His father, Wilfred, worked briefly as a taster in his Uncle Bill's meatball factory and later as a door-to-door door salesman. But business was slow. Most houses already had front doors and people who couldn't afford to buy one either rented one for a few pence a week or bought one on hire purchase, even though this meant they paid hundreds of pounds for something that was only worth a few shillings.

To make ends meet, his mother took in washing from better off families then sold it at cart boot sales. When people came to collect their washing, they switched the lights off and pretended they were out.

Eric's refined and genteel tastes were at odds with those of his uncouth family and he knew from an early age that he didn't belong.[1] He also knew that he

Eric Blunt (1903 - 1998) pictured front left in 1908 with his natural parents and sisters

didn't want to follow in his father's footsteps as a humble door salesman.

He wanted to become a man of letters. He was determined to escape a life of drudgery and create a better life for himself but he was impatient. Ever resourceful, he hit upon a plan. One night, he crept downstairs and hid in Mr Spiegelman's photographic studio, waiting for a suitable family to come along. After four days, tired and hungry, he smuggled himself into a family portrait at a sitting by the Irwells, one of the wealthiest families in the whole of Wigan.[2]

The Irwells rarely saw their children as they each had nannies and attended boarding school, so when young Eric

George Irwell pictured front left in 1909 with his adoptive parents Mr & Mrs Irwell and their family

followed them home, they assumed he must be one of theirs. It was several weeks before they counted their children and realised they had an extra child.

When they challenged him and attempted to disown him, he referred them to the irrefutable photographic evidence that he was one of theirs. The Irwells already had a son called Eric so they changed his name to George. Thus it was that George Irwell was born.

He had his first essay published at the age of six whilst attending Wackford Blunt's School for Young Toffs, where he finished a very creditable joint fourth in English the same year.[3] Here he acquired a taste for cold showers and sneering at boys from less wealthy backgrounds.

Returning home at Christmas, he found the family home empty and a sign in the window which simply said, "Gorn away."[4] He never forgave his adoptive family for this misspelling.

He was back to square one. His real family didn't want him back nor, to be truthful, did he want to go back. Left to

fend for himself, he slept rough and made a few pennies by painting himself white and posing motionless as a statue for hours on end in Mintball Square.

Irwell's searing indictment of Franco's crackdown on drug dens (1938)

He finally found work as a temp, first in a florist's and then a bakery where he progressed from making barmcakes to working on the cupcake production line. But he found the work dull and unrewarding and took to drink to dull the pain of his miserable existence.

He even started to frequent the many opium dens which existed in Wigan at that time. Sacked for making oversize cupcakes, he started writing a weekly magazine which he sold on the streets of Wigan. He could only write two a week as each magazine was hand written but they brought him to the attention of the editor of the *Wigan Argus,* who offered him the job of cub reporter.

Irwell spent most of his time at Wigan Zoo writing dispatches on the progress of Elsie the lioness and her cubs. Fearing that he would lose his job as soon as the cubs became adults, he fabricated his reports and continued to describe them as cubs for the next five years, not knowing that cubs become adult lions after only eighteen months.

But his fears were unfounded. He was a

talented writer and he was promoted to his dream job – that of sports editor, in which capacity he reported on football, rugby league and darts.[5]

The highlight of his career came in 1936, when Real Madrid invited Wigan to play a friendly to celebrate the opening of their new stadium and Irwell was sent to Spain to report on the game.

Irwell's Road To Wigan Peer (1997) charts the writer's rise from the son of a humble door salesman

He was horrified by what he saw there. Not only was Franco's brutal fascist army conducting a war of attrition against the democratically elected regime, but Alberto Sanchez scored a controversial 86th minute penalty for Madrid in a 1-0 defeat of the Lancashire club.

It was a bitter pill to swallow. But it wasn't the result which most upset Irwell. After all, it was only a friendly. Rather, it was Madrid's negative tactics in which they deployed four fixed defenders playing a strict man-to-man marking system, plus a playmaker in the middle of the field who played the ball together with two midfield players cum wingers.

Wigan is very proud of its association with George Irwell

He foresaw that a style of football in which the skills of the individual are subordinate to the team rather than one in which they are allowed to flourish represented a serious

threat and was determined that it should not gain a foothold in what he called "the beautiful game".[6]

He frequently returned to Spain to campaign against what came to be called the *Catenaccio* system and was badly injured when he was attacked by a gang of Madrid supporters armed with sticks of chorizo before a King's Cup game against Barcelona in 1938.

On his return to Britain, Irwell married Camilla Parker-Penn and went to work for the BBC where he scripted some memorable episodes of the popular wartime radio comedy series *There! It's That Monkey Again, Norman!*[7]

He ended his career as co-presenter with Stuart Balls of the popular TV programme, *It's A Cock Up,* in which teams from all over Lancashire competed for colour televisions and pop-up toasters wearing pantomime horse costumes.

In 1996, he was ennobled by the Labour government when they discovered his humble origins but was later stripped of his peerage when he was convicted of expenses fraud.[8]

Footnotes

1. Irwell later wrote that he felt like "a rich boy trapped in the body of a poor boy." The NHS had not yet been invented and class reassignment operations would have been prohibitively expensive for a working class lad from Wigan. He also wrote that his family smelled but he later denied this.

2. The Irwells (pronounced Irlingwall) could trace their history back to the 13th century when the king granted

Roger de Irwell a large parcel of land together with a manor house and swimming pool for allowing him to sleep with one of his sons. They paid for the upkeep of the house and its grounds by running a number of successful businesses including hiring out doors at exorbitant rates and were major investors in the Wigan Casino Bank.

3. *What I did on my holidays* in the Wackford Blunt School for Young Toffs School magazine. George showed a facility for language far beyond his years and regularly composed his own notes excusing him from mathematics lessons. When his teachers discovered this, they paid him tuppence to pen notes excusing them from the First World War.

4. He never found out whether this was deliberate or whether they had simply forgotten to inform him.

5. Irwell was not only an accomplished writer but a talented footballer and prolific goal scorer, too. A tricky, unorthodox left winger, he played a couple of games for Old Wackfordians and was spotted by a scout for Chorley Town for whom he scored a hat-trick on his debut in a 5-2 defeat of Lytham Miners' Welfare. He played 99 games for Chorley Town scoring 123 goals but his career was cruelly cut short by injury. In 1923 he was described by the *Wigan Argus and Messenger* as the finest player of his generation and with incredible foresight in 1924 by the *Wigan Daily Star* as 'the Lionel Messi of his day'.

6. Irwell came to call this style of football 'totalitarian' and campaigned for freedom of expression in football for many years before recanting shortly before his death in 1998.

7. *There! It's That Monkey Again, Norman!* was so popular that the country would come to a standstill as it tuned in each week but public outrage forced its cancellation when it was mistakenly listed in acronym form in the Radio Times due to lack of space. The career of its host, comedian Tommy Hindley, never fully recovered.

8. In 1997, he claimed £65,000 for a bird bath for which he had only paid £15 twelve months earlier insisting that the amount was a fair reflection of the increase in property prices over the previous twelve months.

Irwell's Publications

Irwell spent one summer working in a CCCP tripe restaurant in Parbold. His first published work, *Down & Out in Parbold & Langho* (1933), drew heavily on his experience working in the kitchens, where his main job was clearing away dead rats from work surfaces before the chefs arrived.

Shortly afterwards, he penned a couple of moderately successful novels (*Barmcake Days* won the Chorley & District Literary Festival Award for best first novel in 1934). With the proceeds from this and his second novel, he took an extended holiday in Europe, where he wrote *Keep The Aspidistra Watered* in 1936 (filmed by 20th Century Spatchcock in 1997 with Richard E. Blunt and Helena Jimmy-Carter in the lead roles).

Franco's strict Catholic brutalism made a lasting impression on Irwell, who lamented the closure of the drug dens of southern Spain in his 1938 narrative documentary *Homage to Catatonia*.

His success with *Aspidistra* was followed up with *Coming Up For Cupcakes* in 1939, a haunting novel with a sense of impending war running through it and a nostalgic look back at the cupcakes of the central character's youth.

Irwell had long been concerned about the rise of Communism and during the war had begun work on a major polemical novel. This was published in 1945 as *Animal Magic* and, drawing on his time as a cub reporter, told the story of a young zookeeper who could talk to his charges. This was later filmed as a children's TV series by the BBC, with Johnny Morris-Minor playing the role of the brutal dictator Stalin, but many children failed to recognize the political message of the programme.

After this, Irwell wrote very little other than the occasional essay for magazines such as *The Watcher* and the *Old Statesman*.

He returned to Wigan only once — to receive an honorary citation from St Martins — but was enobled Lord Blunt of Irwell in 1994. This formed the substance for his searing work *Nineteen Ninety-Four* (1995).

Irwell's autobiography, *The Road To Wigan Peer*, was published in 1997 but is currently out of print.

DW BLUNT
& 20th CENTURY
SPATCHCOCK

Throughout the 'golden age' of British films, the name D W Blunt was synonymous with home grown cinema.

A keen actor and dancer, he decided to have a go at making films. He began showing his home movies of people going to work and strolling in the park in their Sunday best at The Odeon, Parbold in 1918, founding 20th Century Blunt the following year.

In 1920, he met Alfred Spatchcock on a trolley bus in Manchester. Spatchcock was a struggling film director working part-time as a conductor to raise cash to fund his films. Blunt was fascinated by Spatchcock and, like so many others, fell under his spell. They remained inseparable for the rest of their lives.[1]

So it was that, in 1921, 20th Century Blunt merged with The Spatchcock Film Company to become 20th Century Spatchcock. The rest, as a media studies lecturer might say, is film history. The operation was based in a huge tripe factory in the Oldham suburb of Hollinwood where incentives had been made available to lure film makers to

DW Blunt: actor, dancer, film producer

boost the local economy. This became known locally as The Tripe Factory.

At first, it was not easy. Filming could only take place at night when the factory workers had gone home.

But with the Spatchcock studio system ensuring a steady flow of talent eager to render unintelligible transatlantic accents into language that was readily accessible to uncompromising northern ears, Blunt and Spatchcock felt sure their policy of remaking classic films for northern audiences was sure to succeed.

But Blunt and Spatchcock couldn't have been more wrong. Their films proved remarkably unpopular with cinema goers. One possible reason for their failure could be that audiences were too sophisticated and just weren't ready for films made with a shaky hand held camera. Another is that they simply couldn't afford to pay 5s to go to the pictures when the average weekly wage was 6d.

But probably the most important reason is that the films were truly awful and were for many years shown in film schools all over the world as the gold standard for how not to make a film.

Celebrated film critic, Norman Barrie, called the musical *Flat Cap* (1938) featuring Fred A Bannister and Ginger Roberts 'an abomination' and *Lancashire Beauty* (1999) 'probably the worst film ever made.' Critics particularly disliked the scene in which 78 year old Hilda Butcher was seen bathing in a tub of mushy peas. More than forty of their films are featured in film critic Paulette Kayli's *101 Worst Films Of All Time*.

20th Century Spatchcock were renowned for their prodigious output and the fast turn-around of their films. Film historians believe they made over 20,000 films, most of which have been destroyed, sometimes by accident but mostly deliberately.

The last few hundred reels were destroyed in a fire in The Tripe Warehouse in 2002 which police believed to be arson committed by film lovers, but there were simply too many suspects and no one was ever convicted.

The Tripe Factory ceased trading on 1 January 2000 when Blunt and Spatchcock decided they could no longer continue making films under the outdated name of 20th Century Spatchcock.

With Ale and Pie (1941) - one of 20th Century Spatchcock's more enduring films (see footnote 2)

True to their tradition, their last film, *All Quiet On Rebecca Front,* was a flop.

Curiously, despite their unpopularity, their films were a commercial success. This was because their production costs were so low (usually less than £100) that they always made a profit.

Blunt and Spatchcock retired to Sri Lanka very wealthy men and lived there for the rest of their lives. In 2011, The Tripe Marketing Board commissioned a project to locate the 'lost' films of 20th Century Spatchcock and this has already unearthed upwards of 300 films.

Blunt & Spatchcock: The Legacy

DW Blunt and Alfred Spatchcock may not be remembered for the quality of their films, but they more than made up for this in quantity.

At one point, they were making as many as six films a day at their studios in Hollinwood, near Oldham. Their first film, *The Stink,* was shot in The Tripe Factory in less than two hours. Then they started filming on location in the immediate vicinity of the factory before moving further afield.

In just one day they made The Mancunian Trilogy - *The Third Mancunian, The Thin Mancunian* and *The Invisible Mancunian*.[3] The latter was a particularly challenging film as they were unable to find an invisible man to play the starring role, despite placing an advert in the *Hollinwood Advertiser*.

The next morning, they filmed on location in Rossendale, shooting *Mr Blunt Goes to Accrington* and *Dirty Rawtenstall Scoundrels*. After a three hour lunch in The Coach and Horses, they filmed *The Wizard Of Oswaldtwistle*.

They then moved north, making *Men In Blackburn* and *Mississippi Burnley* before spending a weekend in Blackpool where they made *Tramspotting* and the first four *Blackpool Rocky* films. They even crossed the Pennines to make *The Grapes Of Rotherham* with a young

George Fleetwood in Turned Out Ince Again (1941) (see footnote 5)

Henry Honda.[4] Their films cover every genre from epics (*Gone With The Window Cleaner*) to horror (*The Cocktail Cabinet of Dr Calamari*) and war (*Fags of Our Fathers*).

To capitalise on the popularity of cowboy films, they invented the north western genre with films such as *Huyton Noon, Once Upon A Time In The North West* and *True Millstone Grit*.

Gradually, their output declined. By the time the studio closed on New Year's Eve 1999, they were making only one film a day. Their films may have been forgotten by the public, but they are still shining examples for students of how not to make a film.

Footnotes

1. Their relationship attracted much speculation. Neither man married and they lived together for most of their lives. Blunt wrote in *Confessions of a Film-Maker*: "For most of our lives we lived like a married couple-we argued a lot and had separate beds." *Confessions of a Film-Maker* is currently out of print.

2. Set in Wigan during Wakes week, *With Ale & Pie* tells the tale of two unemployed miners who decide to spend a few days in Southport with flamboyant Uncle Dickie. They board the wrong train at Wigan North Western station and end up in Blackpool by mistake.

3. The Mancunian series was briefly revived in the 1980s as The Manc series and included *The Manc Who Fell To Earth* (directed by Nicholas Rogue), the wartime costume drama *Mancs* and *The Manc With The Golden*

Gun starring Roger Moron.

4. The actors and actresses who appear in Blunt and Spatchcock's films are known locally as 'The Hollinwood Greats' and include Beryl Flynn, Charles Claughton, Ronald Coalman, Ingrid Burgerking, James Stewpot, David Nivea, Rita Farnworth, Katherine Blackburn, Audrey Blackburn, Charlton Blumenthal, Al Casino, Henry Honda, Jane Honda and Richard E Blunt.

5. Probably the biggest star in the Hollinwood firmament was Wigan-born George Fleetwood. Fleetwood sang comical songs, often filled with innuendo about the penny whistle with which he accompanied himself. *Auntie Nellie's Bloomers* and *Come And Have A Blow On Me Little Penny Whistle* are typical examples.

20th Century Spatchcock
at War

At the outbreak of war, Blunt and Spatchcock avoided conscription on the grounds that they were both devout cowards.

Blunt joined ENSA but was seriously injured and forced to return home after being hit on the head by an empty bottle thrown from the crowd during his performance of scenes from *Swan Lake*.

Spatchcock joined the Army Film and Photographic Unit and, in 1944, was parachuted into France to film the advance of Allied troops through France.

A gust of wind blew him behind enemy lines where he found refuge with the French film-maker Claude Chablis and his family for whom he made films in return for board and lodgings. He made just two films[1] before being handed over to the Nazis who, discovering he was a film-maker, introduced him to the notorious British traitor and stand-up

A scene from Back to the Fuhrer II—British troops retreat under fire from the Germans

comedian, Lord Ha Ha and Max Goebbels Sr.[2]

The Nazis forced Spatchcock to make propaganda films such as *I Know Where I'm Goering, Another Fine Hess, Tie A Yellow Ribbentrop, The Pink Panzer, A Man Called Horst, Back to the Fuhrer I II and III* and *Saving Private Aryan*.[3,4]

Experts believe that the Nazi surrender was accelerated by several months due to the devastating effect Spatchcock's propaganda films had on the morale of the German people.[5,6]

Footnotes

1. They Eat Horses Don't They about his first day in France and *Jeanne de Florette*, the moving tale of a hunchbacked woman who works in a factory packing lettuce leaves.

2. Max Goebbels Snr was the father of Mad Mel star Max Goebbels Jr.

3. The Pink Panzer, about a gay Nazi tank commander, was Spatchcock's most controversial film and was banned throughout Germany apart from Berlin.

4. Critics believe *Back To The Fuehrer I* was easily the best film of the trilogy.

5. The historian David Goering believes Spatchcock was actually a Nazi sympathizer and that his propaganda films were not intentionally bad. Goering believes Hitler lost the will to live during a private screening of *Saving Private Aryan* in his Berlin bunker on 30 April 1945. Conspiracy theorist David Spike believes the man who committed suicide in the Berlin bunker was Ernest Winterbottom, a Preston window cleaner and Hitler look-alike. *Saving Private Aryan* was harshly criticised for being unrealistic, even though it was filmed during the D-Day landings.

6. On his return to Britain, Spatchcock was knighted for his services to the Allied war effort.

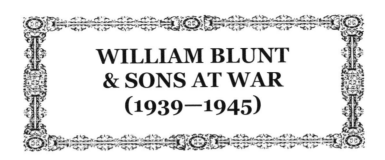

WILLIAM BLUNT
& SONS AT WAR
(1939—1945)

In 1940, times were hard. Essential goods were rationed and there was a thriving black market in bread, sugar, eggs and cupcakes. To make matters worse, supplies of tripe were plentiful.

As a luxury item, fridge magnets were rationed and limited to one per family per week, which was one more than most families wanted.

This led to a glut and prices plummeted. In 1940, you could buy a hundred fridge magnets for less than one halfpenny.

William Blunt & Sons relocated from Wigan to Liverpool to escape the worst of the bombing.[1] The Germans were winning the propaganda war and had commissioned Wilhelm Stumpf und Söhne (Berlin) GmbH to manufacture a range of fridge magnets which the Luftwaffe regularly dropped over many parts of Lancashire.[2]

In 1941, German planes scored a direct hit on William Blunt & Son's Liverpool factory — thought by many to be an act of revenge for the cancellation of Hitler's

The Germans employed increasingly sophisticated propaganda techniques with a series of fridge magnets dropped over Lancashire in 1941

Less sophisticated techniques were employed as the war waged on

lucrative contract as the face of Uncle Bill's Meatballs five years earlier.

The factory was almost completely destroyed and the workers were understandably shaken but, with typical Lancashire phlegm caused by the moist climate, the company ordered its employees to 'keep calm and carry on

William Blunt & Sons workers were exhorted to Carry On Making Fridge Magnets during World War Two

making fridge magnets' and put a huge poster on the wall to this effect.

The company at this time was under the stewardship of Talcott William Blunt, third son of its founder, William Gladstone. Blunt wrote to Churchill asking him to pay a morale-boosting visit to the factory but Churchill was unavailable due to a prior commitment. His secretary referred Blunt instead to the Harvey Clegg Look-Alike Agency in Childwall.

Herbert Wilfred Duckworth was normally employed as a Neville Chamberlain look-alike but bookings had dropped off after Chamberlain resigned as prime minister.

Herbert Duckworth, Ernest Winterbottom and Albert Gradewell were never idle during the war. Demand for Duckworth's Churchill's appearances was unremitting, despite his obviously poor resemblance to the British PM.

John Harvey Clegg pressed Duckworth into accepting bookings as Churchill due to unprecedented demand for morale boosting visits by the prime minister, despite the fact that Duckworth was tall and skinny and bore no resemblance whatsoever to Churchill, even when wearing a homburg and smoking a fat cigar.

It is for this reason that Duckworth's visit to the bombed factory had no discernible effect on morale. However, he was impressed by the poster displayed on the one remaining factory wall and this resulted in Blunt receiving a

Hitler look-alike Ernest Winterbottom rarely escaped the prying eyes of photographers, even when trying to relax for an hour or two on Southport beach

government commission to produce a range of patriotic fridge magnets for the German and domestic markets to counteract the effects of Nazi propaganda.

Britain hit back with its own magnet drops over northern Germany in 1942

Such was the importance attached to winning the propaganda war that munitions were melted down to provide the metal for the fridge magnets which were given away everywhere, from vendors on street corners to usherettes in cinemas.

Families would huddle round their

Stars of stage and screen rallied round to support the war effort

fridges of an evening listening to the radio and looking at their fridge magnets which displayed patriotic messages often endorsed by stars of stage, screen and sport such as Beryl Flynn.[3]

But it wasn't all fridge magnet-making for the Blunt family. Mention must be made of dashing Captain WE 'Bomber' Blunt and his young friend, Ginger, who successfully completed 243 bombing missions, including the destruction of the Berlin factory of Wilhelm Stumpf und Söhne (Berlin) GmbH.[4,5]

Wilhelm Stumpf und Söhne GmbH in June, 1944

Ironically, when the war ended, it was Wilhelm Stumpf who thrived. Without the hindrance of a fridge magnet tax and with the benefit of huge investment in plant and machinery (principally from the US), they were in a position to capitalise on Europe's post-war hunger for fridge magnets.

After the war, the German fridge magnet industry benefited from massive investment in new factories, as this company brochure from the 1960s demonstrates

Wilhelm Stumpf und Söhne GmbH

Footnotes

1. This proved to be a huge tactical mistake by the company. Wigan remained remarkably unscathed during the war while Liverpool was heavily bombed.

2. Controversy surrounds the part played by Wilhelm Stumpf und Söhne (Berlin) GmbH during the war. An official company history discovered by noted historian AJP Blunt in 1962 has the pages covering the years 1936 to 1945 missing.

3. The most popular programmes were the many cookery programmes which made up much of the BBC radio output at that time; *There! It's That Monkey Again, Norman!* and *Mintball Square*, the long running soap opera which followed the lives and loves of characters such as Elsie Stunner, Ken Marlow and

Das Auto der Zukunft. Heute.

'The car of tomorrow. Today.' A 1986 East German magnet advertising the latest model of the Trabant which had all the latest features including lockable doors and a clutch.

Albert Spatchcock.[2]

4. There is some controversy over the bombing of the factory which was situated in Berlin, 150 miles away from Hamburg docks, the mission's prime target. It is widely believed that the decision to bomb the factory was taken by Capt Blunt for commercial reasons and as an act of revenge for the bombing of his uncle's factory in Liverpool.

5. A state of the art factory was constructed in 1945 on the site of the factory destroyed during the war[1] and by 1952 Wilhelm Stumpf und Söhne were producing over 200,000 fridge magnets a year, making them the biggest manufacturers of fridge magnets in the world.[3]

Sub-Footnotes

1. The factory straddled the border between capitalist West Berlin and communist East Berlin and when the Berlin Wall went up in 1962, the factory was effectively split in two. This caused problems, particularly as the toilets were located in East Berlin. It wasn't until the Berlin Wall came down in 1989 that the workers could go to the toilet without having to go through passport control .

2. An episode of *Welder's Playtime* hosted by Tommy Hindley and featuring Lynette Vera and Beryl Flynn was recorded in the canteen of William Blunt & Sons' factory in 1942, but no recording survives.

3. Between 1960 and 1989, the western part of the factory employed six workers and produced over 2 million magnets per year whilst the eastern part of the factory employed 250 workers and produced 700 magnets per year.

TRIPE —
FOOD OF THE GODS

Ask any Lancastrian what The Tripe Factory means to them and the reply might well be "Hollinwood", or perhaps "Alfred Spatchcock" or, most likely, "What the heck are you talking about?"

But there's a lot more to The Tripe Factory than the films of Alfred Spatchcock.

It can also refer to a factory where tripe - the first or second stomach of a ruminant (particularly an ox) - is processed.

Tripe was once the staple diet of the industrial towns of Lancashire, a cheap and nourishing food which played an important part in making the north west the engine room of Britain.

In 1920, for example, there were an estimated 2,000 tripe shops and restaurants in Wigan alone and something like half a million in Lancashire. In fact, many family firms did nothing but boil and sell tripe, cowheel and trotters.

Its popularity can be put down to many

The abandoned former tripe factory in Hollinwood where Blunt and Spatchcock made their first films. There are few clues that this now derelict site was once such a powerhouse of British film production.

things. First and foremost, it was cheap and filling: you could feed a family of 6 for less than a farthing. Last, but not least, it was versatile and could be put to many other uses such as an inexpensive floor covering, upholstering material or for cleaning windows.

At the height of its popularity in the 30s and 40s, the tripe jump was the flagship event of the Lancashire Games and made up a quarter of the Lancashire triathlon, alongside black pudding throwing and synchronised darts.

During the war when fabrics were scarce, women would make clothes from tripe and throughout Lancashire there arose large numbers of tripe dressers (often back-room businesses) who dressed women in the finest garments made of tripe.

Probably the first to dress in this way was Lady Ha Ha, wife of the notorious traitor Lord Ha Ha, who caused a sensation when she wore a magnificent off the shoulder white dress made from the finest Lancashire tripe at the opening ceremony of the 1936 Olympic Games in Berlin.

Albert Grimshaw was Burnley's finest tripe jumper and won gold medals in the 1932 and 1936 Lancashire Games

One major chain of shops in Lancashire, Chorley Co-operative Cattle Products, not only sold tripe but ran restaurants selling a wide variety of cooked tripe dishes. Their processing factory near Chorley was one of the largest of its type. At the height of its popularity in the 30s, CCCP had a shop selling cow products with a café in the back on almost every corner and over 100 exclusive tripe restaurants, some of which were surprisingly ornate.

Its flagship restaurant on Market Street, Manchester, was a magnificent art deco building outside which there would often be queues, despite the fact that it had seating for 200 diners. Waiters dressed in evening suits would serve staple dishes such as stewed tripe and onions as well as speciality dishes such as Tripe Wellington (tripe served in a rubber boot). Less discerning diners would throw the tripe away and eat the Wellington.

The Market Street restaurant was a firm favourite with the stars of Alfred Spatchcock's Hollinwood film studios who would often visit between takes during filming of movies. In the 30s, it was the place to see and be seen.

The interior of Manchester's Market Street CCCP restaurant, now sadly demolished

CCCP's popularity is attributable to the fact that their restaurants were known to be pest-free. You could dine there safe in the knowledge that the kitchens would be free from rats and cockroaches as they couldn't stand the smell of the stuff.

CCCP's distinctive logo had to be abandoned in 1936 after fascist attacks

In 1952, readers of one Lancashire newspaper were offered the chance to win the weight of their baby in tripe in an attempt to revive flagging sales

Their shops and restaurants are probably best remembered for their distinctive red shop fronts with a yellow 'sickle and hammer' logo which led many people to believe mistakenly that it was connected with the Soviet Union. This was completely unfounded but led to regular attacks on its shops by fascists.[1] In 1936, CCCP was forced to rebrand when the windows of its Manchester Market Street restaurant were smashed by a gang led by vegetarian fascist leader, Oswald Muesli.[2]

Writer George Irwell was a frequent visitor to the CCCP restaurant in Mintball Square in Wigan and could often be seen sitting in the window tucking into a dish of tripe or trotters, writing his novels. It was here that he is thought to have penned the immortal lines:

Bring me my slippers
Bring me my pipe
And bring me a steaming bowl of tripe

Consumption of tripe started to decline after the war due to the ending of rationing, the advent of the welfare state and increasing affluence — despite the use of competitions such as Win The Weight of Your Baby in Tripe launched with a fanfare in the *Wigan Daily Mail* in 1952.[3]

In the 70s, the Tripe Marketing Board (previously The Association For The Legal Disposal Of Unwanted Cow Products) was established to revive its flagging fortunes with the post-ironic slogan *You Either Loathe it or Hate It.*

The Tripe Marketing Board has adopted post-irony in an attempt to revive sales

The TMB later encouraged retailers to open drive throughs and takeaways such as Tripe Hut and Tripeland to compete with burger and pizza fast food restaurants and they enjoyed some success in the Lancashire heartlands, particularly when they introduced a mascot, Timothy Tripe.

At first sight, Timothy Tripe was a perfectly innocent-looking pantomime cow. But when he stood on his hind legs to smoke a cigarette or enjoy a refreshing pint of beer, the insides of his stomach would be revealed with the entrails dangling as if the cow had undergone some form of brutal medieval torture, terrifying children and adults alike.

Timothy Tripe was abandoned after just two weeks when a student wearing the costume outside the restaurant in Mintball Square, Wigan was savagely attacked by a Jack Russell.

Tripe has enjoyed something of a revival, ever since punk chef Gary Ginnel published a tripe recipe in his book *Cooking With Gaz* (2006) and celebrity chef Richard Charnock served tripe ice cream with black pudding sauce at *The Fat Cow*, his Michelin starred restaurant in Chorley.

Other chefs such as Marco Pierre Blunt, Jamie Fagin and the Bald Cyclists have jumped on the bandwagon, but the Tripe Marketing Board had to deal with a major PR disaster in 2009 when vegetarian model Katie Cutprice collapsed and had to be put on a respirator when she was forced to eat a plate of tripe as part of the Foul Food Challenge on the popular TV programme, *I'm Famous — Put A Wasp In My Mouth*.

She swore so much that at least two elderly viewers collapsed and the programme had to be taken off air for 20 minutes. Subsequent series dropped tripe in favour of elephant testicles and snake vomit.

Skilful media management by the TMB meant that this unfortunate episode wasn't allowed to interfere with the tripe renaissance.4 Local investment agencies across the north west are reported to be preparing to spend heavily in the tripe sector. Once again, Lancashire may be about to take the lead!

Timothy Tripe, briefly the mascot of the Tripe Marketing Board

Footnotes

1. CCCP blamed their advertising agency Spaatchcock and Spaatchcock for the confusion. They paid rival agency Bootle Boggle Pegotty £250,000 to come up with a new brand and logo. The hamster on a cycle was not a success so they reverted to their original branding.

2. The sickle represented the grass on which the cows fed whilst the hammer was the preferred instrument with which they were dispatched at most reputable abattoirs

2. Despite its popularity, tripe has often polarised opinion and been the butt of jokes. Comedian Bernard Manningham, who based his entire routine on jokes about tripe, once said that a sheet of tripe could often be found hanging in many outside toilets in case there was a shortage of newspaper and that tripe restaurants were pest-free because rats would commit suicide rather than eat it.

3. The Tripe Marketing Board scored an unlikely success in 1972 when independent film-maker Morgan Spatchcock made *Supertripe Me*, a documentary which followed the drastic effects on his physical and psychological well-being of only eating cow products. Spatchcock dined at CCCP restaurants three times a day for 30 days, eating every item on the chain's menu at least once including tripe, cows' heels, pigs' trotters, lamb's fry, tongue, brains, elder, wessel, genitals and anus. The film had the opposite effect to that intended. Although Spatchcock went completely bald and lost the use of his arms and legs as a result of the experiment, he also lost two stones in weight. Thousands of overweight Lancashire women went on tripe-only diets and tripe sales rocketed. The film was discredited by the TMB when it emerged that Spatchcock was a member of a radical vegetarian movement dedicated to the elimination of tripe from the human diet and that the supposed side effects were fabricated.

FISH & CHIPS:
A MARRIAGE MADE
IN FLEETWOOD

If there is one meal which has almost come to rival tripe and onions as the national dish of the county of Lancashire, then it is fish and chips.

Few would disagree with Professor Richard Parkinson, Emeritus Professor of Atheism and Fishing at the University of Fleetwood, that the fish and chips one can buy today in any chip shop has evolved from raw fish and potatoes over millions of years.[1]

But just how fish and chips came together in such a perfect marriage has puzzled historians for centuries.

According to an old Lancashire legend, when Bonnie Prince Charlie marched south with his army to claim the British throne in 1745, he stopped at Blackpool for the weekend.

In the army's baggage train were vast quantities of whisky and tins of shortbread with which his soldiers sustained themselves. They also carried huge cooking pots in which the army chefs would deep fry any local produce

Fanny Blunt, the Fleetwood Fisherwife (left) and as depicted in a statue on Fleetwood seafront

they could find.[2]

In the village of Bispham[3] just outside Blackpool, they came across a huge field of potatoes which they picked, sliced and deep fried together with some fresh fish they caught in the abundant waters of the Irish Sea.

The Blunt Family Archive, however, suggests a very different version of events. Fanny Blunt was the niece of William Gladstone and Ernestina Blunt. At the age of 16 she fell pregnant by an Irish potato salesman[4] who told her he had to return to Ireland on an urgent family matter.

Cast out of the family home, she made her way to Fleetwood to await the return of her lover and could often be seen on the esplanade looking out to sea wearing just a cloak and some Wellington boots.

Penniless and homeless, she would gather fish from the sea and walk the streets of Fleetwood with a hand basket selling her produce accompanied by her daughter, Molly. She became known as the Fleetwood Fishwife.[5]

The proprietor of a local chip shop, Henry Rumsden, took pity on her and offered her board and lodgings in return for help in his chip shop. They began to sell Fanny's raw fish as an accompaniment to Henry's chips, wrapped in copies of *The Fleetwood Bugle*.

But locals were not accustomed to raw fish and found it unpalatable. Customers would eat the delicious chips but throw the fish away and read the newspaper.[6]

One day, while Fanny was giving the shop a bit of a makeover, one of the live fish jumped into a bucket containing some flour and water wallpaper paste and then into the hot oil in which the chips were frying.

Fanny tried to rescue the fish but it was too late. She was heartbroken. But the death of the fish had a silver lining. It tasted delicious deep fried in batter and the dish proved extremely popular with their customers, particularly served with a portion of chips and some dried marrowfat peas soaked overnight in water then simmered with a little sugar and salt until they formed a thick green lumpy 'soup'.[7]

Fanny and Henry married and prospered, moved back to Wigan and opened a chain of fish and chip shops across Lancashire which was second only in popularity to the CCCP chain of tripe restaurants.

Footnotes

1. *The Shellfish Gene*, currently out of print.

2. Bonnie Prince Charlie's army eventually ran out of cooking oil at Derby and returned to Scotland.

3. Bispham is named from the old Norse: 'Bisp' meaning cold-sore and 'ham' meaning village, hence 'village of the people with cold sores'.

4. The Irish potato salesman was actually Michael O'Laoghaire, a Birkdale shopkeeper who was married with four children.

5. The story of Fanny Blunt the Fleetwood fishwife is told in the novel *The Irish Potato Salesman's Woman* by John Chickens.

6. It did, however, prove popular with Japanese tourists holidaying in nearby Blackpool.

7. In an attempt to revive flagging sales of tripe in the 70s, CCCP experimented with deep-fried battered tripe with onion fritters as a take-away dish but it was not popular, even with Japanese tourists.

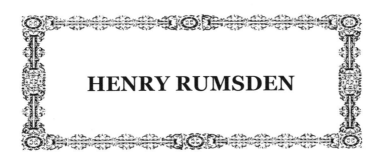

HENRY RUMSDEN

Henry Rumsden's first fish & chip shop in Wigan opened at number 48 Mintball Square in 1908 and was a popular place for locals to congregate for almost eight decades before it closed in 1986.

Henry Rumsden was something of a marketing genius and managed to convince generations of fish and chip consumers that his product was superior to all others. In time, a chain of shops opened up as far afield as Billinge and Ashton-in-Makerfield and the name Henry Rumsden became synonymous with high prices and queues.

Sometime in 1912/13, it is reputed that Adolf Hitler, then just a young housepainter from Austria, spent two weeks working as a casual fish fryer at the Upholland branch of Rumsden's. There is only limited circumstantial evidence to this effect — a piece of graffiti carved onto the old wooden counter saying *'Adolf war hier'* was fortunately photographed by Mr Giles Cobham of Chorley before the counter was later destroyed — but it is known that Hitler was in the north west visiting

Henry Rumsden's Fish & Chip Shop, Mintball Square, c1972

family members at this time.[1]

Despite opening branches elsewhere, the spiritual home of Rumsden's was always Mintball Square, at least until one fateful night in June 1986.

In the 1980s, sales of fish and chips had started to decline as more attractive takeaways such as pizzas and hamburgers had increased in popularity. Jack Rumsden, the then manager of the family firm, realised that to compete with these new foodstuffs they would have to radically reduce their costs. Local press reports from the time suggest that Rumsden hit upon the profitable idea of substituting the hitherto inedible Blunt fish (a variety of Asian Wrasse that was both cheap and plentiful) for the more popular cod and haddock.

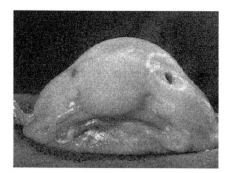

The Blunt fish

During experiments in his garden shed, Jack had discovered that marinating the Blunt fish in methylated spirits for half an hour could make it reasonably palatable.

Unfortunately, Rumsden reckoned without the flammable properties of methylated spirits and, within days of the launch of his new product, the entire premises - and many of those adjacent - were consumed in a vast fire. Fortunately, no one was seriously hurt but it led to the closure of a number of popular businesses on the Square.

The 'Rumsden Disaster' (which co-incided with the annual Bluntsday celebrations in Wigan) effectively sounded the death-knell for Mintball Square, although a much more useful car park has since been built on the site.

Henry Rumsden, c1950

Henry Rumsden's c1986

Site of Henry Rumsden's c1995

Footnotes

1. An alternative theory suggests that the Hitler in question was none other than Mr Harold Pittington, a Hitler look-alike who was on the books of the Jabez Cowell Agency in New Brighton. Mr Pittington was assassinated by a renegade faction of the Waffen SS whilst on a gateaux tasting holiday in the Black Forest in 1933, so this theory was never corroborated. The real Hitler was visiting his aunt in Liverpool and thus escaped death.

THE BLUNT FAMILY

 Timothy William Blunt
1880 – 1937

 Robert Falcon Blunt
1881 – 1912

 Talcott Blunt
1881 – 1956

 Walter Blunt
1882 – 1965

 William Henry Blunt
1883 – 1940

 William Rochester Blunt
1884 – 1922

 JMW Blunt
1885 – 1937

 George Bernard Blunt
1887 – 1948

 Thomas William Witold Blunt
1889 – 1942

 John Boynton Blunt
1894 – 1984

 John Henry Blunt
1897 – 1920

 David Wark Blunt
1899 – 2004

 Henry Ossett Blunt
1899 – 1922

 AJP Blunt
1906 – 2012

The full extent of the influence of the fourteen children of William Gladstone Blunt and his wife Ernestina Fleetwood has not yet been fully documented.

Before his untimely death early in 2012, AJP Blunt was said to be contemplating a definitive history of the Blunt family. Alas, time was not on his side. However, even a cursory leaf through the Blunt Archive reveals that they have left their indelible mark on the bed sheet of history.

There is no room here to document the descendents of those children - people like Cilla, Jeffrey or DH Blunt, for example. Their story will have to await a further volume.

In the meantime, there follow some brief biographical details of the Blunt family members (with the exception of John Henry and DW Blunt, who have been covered earlier in this volume), to give readers a flavour of their contribution to history.

It is sincerely hoped that this will be of use to academics, local historians and to the general reader and that in the fullness of time more will be learned and shared.

TIMOTHY BLUNT

Timothy William Blunt (left, right) was the first child of William Gladstone and Ernestina Blunt - a visionary who saw an opportunity to make his mark in Wigan as a chemist.

Demand for all manner of quack remedies in Wigan was high and at first his business did well. Within three years of opening his first shop in Mintball Square, Timothy was considering opening another shop in nearby Ince. But as visionary as he was, Timothy Blunt was also cautious.

He had employed an assistant chemist, a Mr Jesse Foot from Nottingham, but grew increasingly perturbed when Jesse began dressing like him and mimicking his mannerisms.

There were those in Wigan who claimed not to be able to tell them apart. Others thought they might be brothers. Worried that Jesse might be plotting to take over his nascent empire, Timothy sacked him.[1]

Timothy became even more cautious when he noticed that Jesse had erased the apostrophe in the sign above his shop. He dropped plans for a second shop and even spurned an offer from Gerald Fenniwragg to partner him in the production of his patent bile tablets.

When Timothy died in 1948, his daughter kept the shop open and effected some modernisation. But trade was not good. The writing was on the wall for Blunts the Chemist and closure was almost inevitable.[2]

ROBERT FALCON BLUNT

Robert Falcon Blunt, explorer extraordinaire, was certainly the most adventurous of William and Ernestina Blunt's children and is probably best remembered for his failed expedition to the magnetic North Pole in 1913.

He positioned his base camp in the rear garden of his cousins, Dagmar and Gudrun Bløntvik. From here he intended to sledge over the packed ice throughout the arctic winter to be the first person to plant a flag on the magnetic North Pole.

Captain Blunt estimated that the return trek would take no more than 93 days but the expedition carried food for 140, 'just in case' as he put it in an early diary entry. Sadly, as we now know, his plans were thwarted.

As Dagmar later told reporters, "We got worried about the milk bottles that were piling up outside the hut so we eventually opened the door and could not believe our eyes. Seated at a tiny, flimsy table was Robert, with a pen in his hand and in the truckle beds that lined the tent were the bodies of the entire team - all dead."

Captain Blunt and his team were doomed to failure the moment they established base camp. The Bløntviks had opened the most northerly of William Blunt & Sons fridge magnet shops. Their basement, stretching deep into their back garden, housed over 32 tons of stock - a magnetic force three times greater than that of the North Pole.

It is now known that Captain Blunt had set off each day using familiar landmarks to guide him. As these ran out, he had to rely on his navigator's compass which led him inexorably and tragically back to his base camp tent, situated as it was over the vast pile of magnetic matter.[1,2]

TALCOTT W BLUNT (& OLAV QUISLING)

Talcott Blunt was born in 1883, the third son of William Gladstone and Ernestina Blunt. From an early age he had a practical bent and could often be found in his father's shed playing with his tools.

It came as no surprise to his family, therefore, when he left school and opened a hardware shop on Mintball Square. Unfortunately, it did not thrive, possibly because he was charging too much, the range of stock was too limited or (as some have suggested) because *Blunt Tools* was not the best choice of name for a hardware store.

One evening, as he was shutting up shop, a Norwegian sailor, who had become separated from his shipmates on a night out in Wigan, came in with a broken compass, looking for a screw. Quisling saw immediately how the ailing business could be improved.[1] In 1911, Blunt and Quisling was born. The shop slowly built up a reputation based on a philosophy of selling good quality products at a fair price.[2]

Encouraged by this success, Blunt & Quisling moved to a new warehouse a couple of miles outside town on the A577 with parking for up to 150 horse drawn carriages. But the new business struggled. They had not taken into account the fact that few people owned their own transport and the No 42 Wigan to Ormskirk horse-bus only ran once a day.

They asked advertising experts Spaatchcock and Spaatchcock to come up with some ideas to revitalise the business. On their advice they changed the name of the business to Quisling and Blunt. When this had no effect they shortened it to Q&B, but the business closed in 1987, the victim of strong local competition.[3]

Footnotes

TIMOTHY BLUNT

1. Foot left to pursue a career as a door-to-door door salesman and was never heard of again.

2. Even the purchase of one of those little lime green weighing machines to position outside the shop was not enough. Blunts closed in 1987, too early to take advantage of the generous compulsory purchase scheme operated by Wigan council when much of Mintball Square was finally demolished.

ROBERT FALCON BLUNT

1. Blunt's diary explains the circumstances : 'Great God, this is an awful place. Once again, after setting forth in hope and expectation only ten hours ago, we are back where we started. What superior force brings us back nightly to our embarkation point? No-one is more skilled in following a compass than our navigator, yet every day we finish where we started.'

2. A strict disciplinarian, Blunt remained in total control of his team. All other members were later found to have been executed. Blunt's diary again: 'More insubordination today. Able Seaman Jones complained of frost bite in both feet and said that, as we returned to the exact place from whence we started every day, he would prefer to sit in the tent and await our return. I cannot permit such talk, which could infect the minds of the others, so I carried him outside and shot him."

TALCOTT W BLUNT

1. Olav Quisling was from a long line of Scandinavian hardware retailers who had built up a reputation not only for the quality of their products but for the attention they gave to cost control, operational details and continuous product development. Blunt had a soft spot for sailors, anyway and invited the Norwegian to become his business partner. Quisling bought a half share in the business and never returned to his ship.

2. House prices were booming and DIYers and property investors alike flocked to the shop from as far away as Hindley and Appley Bridge.

3. Q&B failed to recapture the success of their early Mintball Square days. Even opening a small café where they served Uncle Bill's Meat-Free Meatballs in a tasty Norwegian cod sauce failed to attract customers. They limped on until finally closing in 1987, when a more modern establishment was opened a few miles up the road in Warrington by a hitherto unknown Swedish retailer.

LORD PARKER OF PARBOLD (WALTER BLUNT)

Where to begin with Lord Parker of Parbold, probably the most enigmatic member of the Blunt family?

Poet, philosopher, inventor, soldier, statesman, sporting hero, adventurer, novelist. He was none of these yet he built a very successful career convincing the Lancashire public that he was. According to his authorised biography,[1] Timothy Parker was educated at Wackford Blunt's School for Young Toffs, Oxford, Cambridge and the Sorbonne. Conscripted into the army in 1898, he fought at the Battle of Damon Hill and was awarded the Victoria Cross for bravery before returning to Lancashire, where he pursued a successful career as a multi-talented sportsman.[2]

He married Winifred Higgins,[3] and became MP for Wigan (North Western) before being ennobled for services to humanity after inventing a prototype for the tea bag.

However, careful study of The Blunt Family Archive reveals that Lord Timothy Parker was actually born plain Walter Blunt, a humble bank clerk and fantasist. Blunt made a fortune investing in proper tea but lost it in the price crash of 1905. He turned to writing fiction and dashed off a novel one afternoon which became an overnight success —*Adam and Eve*.[4]

Blunt made a fortune from this and other potboilers and moved to a luxury penthouse apartment overlooking the Leeds-Liverpool canal where he continued to write, convincing himself and members of the public that Lord Timothy Parker was a real person. He spent the last years of his life in a psychiatric hospital.

WILLIAM HENRY BLUNT

William Henry Blunt was the fifth child of William Gladstone and Ernestina Blunt and very much the runt of the family. As an adult he never grew much beyond five feet in height and as a schoolboy was even smaller.

Growing up, William had all the usual interests of a teenager of the period. He traded football cards, spotted trains and tried to assemble a collection of contemporary adult images. With his height set firmly against him, Blunt was unable to reach the top shelf of any newsagent in Wigan, so his own collection of images consisted mainly of pages culled from the ladies' undergarment section of mail order catalogues (although he was fortunate to receive some racy postcards from Naples when his Uncle Herbert undertook the Grand Tour in 1897).

Shamefaced, he watched his friends boast of their impressive collections of magazines featuring ladies clad only in their vests and bloomers, while inside he was smarting with indignity and embarrassment. Desperate for adult entertainment, he decided to set up his own newsagents. He opened a stall at Wigan Wallgate Station and it wasn't long before he was able to open up his first proper shop.[1]

From the start, William set out to be different, determined that no other teenage boy should suffer the same humiliation as he. He shocked contemporary Wigan by displaying copies of *Gentlemen Only* and *Big Ankles* at eye level.

Following a high-profile court appearance for indecency, Blunt was imprisoned for two years. He sold his shop to Mr Rupert Murdstone in 1903 and died in 1940, a broken man.

WILLIAM ROCHESTER BLUNT

William Gladstone Blunt sired fourteen children to his wife, Ernestina - or did he? That was the question family members were forced to confront in 1922 when a fifteenth child appeared on the scene determined to claim her share of the family fortune.

Cordelia Blunt, for whom no birth certificate was ever found, claimed to have been born in 1884 and insisted that she was the twin sister of William Rochester Blunt. Rochester shared his father's enthusiasm for invention but none of his business acumen and became increasingly determined to wrest control of the company.

He confined himself to a secluded house in Orrell Park with only Winnie Pegg, the family's aged retainer. Although intensely loyal, Winnie was by this stage scarcely able to look after herself and her 300 elks (owing to some confusion on the part of the Canadian Wildlife Fund, lame elks were regularly delivered to the house). Rochester conceived an audacious plan and created 'Cordelia'. Dressing himself as a woman about town and with an improbably high pitched voice, Cordelia presented herself at the monthly film showings at Blunt Towers as Rochester's twin sister, presumed still-born.

Although initially opinion was divided about Cordelia's claim, she easily passed the battery of tests about family history, so the Blunts were forced to concede that she was indeed a long-lost family member. Buoyed by this success, Rochester was about to begin the next phase of his plan, the invention of fourteen more brothers and sisters who would then hold the majority vote, when disaster struck and the family was reduced to thirteen. News was received that Cordelia (and then Rochester) had been gored to death by an elk.[1,2]

Footnotes

WALTER BLUNT

1. *The Greatest Man Who Ever Lived* was published in 1953 but is currently out of print.

2. In 1900, he opened the batting for Lancashire against the Australian tourists at Old Trafford,[1] the following day competing in The Lancashire Games, winning gold medals in the marathon, synchronized darts and tripe jump.

3. He successfully defended a tiny garrison against 10,000 Zulus single handed whilst his fellow soldiers had their lunch.

4. Winifred Higgins was twice winner of the Miss Elegant, Fragrant and Radiant Lancashire competition and an occasional model for *Big Ankles* magazine.

5. Blunt had hit upon a formula for success which he repeated endlessly in his hundreds of books, sometimes only changing the title of the book and the name of the characters.[2] He went on to write hundreds of potboilers about Lord Timothy Parker, an enigmatic adventurer and amateur sleuth who solves crimes whilst opening the batting for Lancashire and writing potboilers.[3,4]

Sub-Footnotes

1. Parker scored a double century before lunch, taking nine Australian wickets for four runs in the afternoon session.

2. The formula he had stumbled upon was one the avid bibliophiles of Lancashire couldn't get enough of-crime, romance and tripe.

3. Dorothy L Greggs is said to have based the character of Lord Peter Wimpey on Lord Timothy Parker.

4. His books include *Samson and Delilah, Abraham and Sarah, Hosea and Gomer, Moses and Miriam, Boaz and Ruth* and *Martha and Lazarus*. His books are all currently out of print.

WILLIAM HENRY BLUNT

1. William attended an evening class in the science of selling newspapers run by Mr Rupert Murdstone at the St Helens branch of the Capitalists' Education Association. He lost a fortune with his ill-fated enterprise: much of the money was lost on purchasing stock since Wigan at that time boasted over two dozen daily newspapers, none with a circulation of more than 200. These included *The Wigan Courier, The Wigan Argus, The Wigan and Parbold Standard*[1], *The Parbold and Wigan Clarion* and the *Wigan Daily Mail*.[1]

2. William's disused shop in Mintball Square was subsequently taken over by a Mr. Desmond Rich as the Wigan outlet for his own chain of *Privateer* shops which specialised in risqué magazines. It operated profitably until 1995 when it was demolished following a fire in a nearby fish and chip shop.

Sub-Footnote

1. In 1905, *The Wigan and Parbold Standard* merged with *The Wigan Argus* to become *The Wigan and Parbold Standard & Argus*.

WILLIAM ROCHESTER BLUNT

1. Fanny Blunt's diary reveals all: 17th June 1922 'It is with great sadness that I write these words. Cousin Cordelia is dead. I know not how her death occurred. A telegram arrived at 4.30 this afternoon with the news that Cordelia's body had been found on the A566 in Orrell Park. I can only surmise that she was going to visit her dear brother Rochester. I do not know the full details, only that she was gored to death by an angry elk. I will miss her cheery disposition and I love the way that she did not care what people thought about her facial hair or her flat-chestedness. I wish I could be so carefree about my own problems in this area.'

2. Prior to going to bed, Fanny completed the day's diary: 'Dear diary, I will mark this day forever as the blackest ever in the history of our family. News has arrived that our cousin, Rochester, has also been mangled to death by an elk. As a mark of respect, George Bernard has vowed to withdraw the series of elk magnets from all outlets with immediate effect.'

93

JMW BLUNT

Joseph Mallard William Blunt was the seventh child of William and Ernestina and it was clear to his parents that young Joseph had artistic pretensions from an early age.

After school he was encouraged by his parents to enrol in an acting classes after school with a view to a career on the stage. But his early theatre experiences were not encouraging - young Joseph's performance in Andrew Lloyd-Grossman's musical adaptation of *The Old Co-Op Shop* was described by critics as 'sullen'.

He took up sketching as a hobby and moved onto watercolours a few years later. At this point his remarkable facility for painting trains at night was discovered. He began to specialise in trains in tunnels, working at various locations (mainly in east Lancashire) to sharpen his talent.[1]

His 1899 classic *The 18.45 in the Brooksbottom Tunnel* was widely acclaimed as one of the most successful of the genre, although making the sketches for the work almost cost him his life. The public — initially fascinated to try to discern the trains in the dark of the tunnels — soon became bored by Blunt's work with its repeated theme of pitch-blackness. He eventually gave up painting and for a few years earned a living as a sub-postmaster in Colne. JMW Blunt died without issue in 1937.

JMW Blunt's
The 18.45 in the
Brooksbottom Tunnel

GEORGE BERNARD BLUNT

George Bernard Blunt was a prolific Wigan playwright who reputedly penned over 600 stage dramas, the vast majority of which remain unperformed to this day.[1]

His writings address complex social themes such as marriage, religion and fridge magnet manufacturing. He was the eighth child of William Gladstone and Ernestina Blunt and, though not directly involved in fridge magnet manufacture himself, he proposed the launch of a range of inter-war designs promoting radical politics, many of which are still in production.

Blunt was an ardent socialist and was angered by what he saw as the exploitation of the working class. He became an accomplished orator until a poor quality denture fitting made him almost unintelligible to all but his closest friends.

Along with Fabios Sidney and Beatrice Websyte, he established the Wigan School of Home Economics, which was to prove influential in the development of cupcakes in the 1920's and down to the present day.

In 1931, Blunt and his colleagues from the WSHE visited the Soviet Union, returning as apologists for 'Uncle Joe' Stalin. Inspired by the Great War success of Uncle Bill's Meat-Free Meatballs, they set about production of Uncle Joe's Rice Balls.[2]

Despite extensive advertising, the Rice Balls never really took off and GB Blunt retired to obscurity in Billinge.

THOMAS BLUNT

Thomas William Witold Blunt was born in 1889, the ninth child of William and Ernestina Blunt.

Whilst his siblings were content with staying close to home, from an early age Thomas was often to be found travelling around the area, sometimes as far afield as Leigh and Standish. He made the most of his Supersaver card which allowed almost unlimited travel on the local omnibus services.

It probably came as no great surprise to his family, therefore, when he set himself up as a travel agent, organising conducted tours to neighbouring towns such as Aspull and Ince. His tours were initially very popular with locals but Thomas learnt the hard way that in the travel business tastes are fickle.

He lost customers to rival companies which organised excursions to more exotic locations such as Birkdale and Lytham St Annes. It was a bitter pill to swallow. Fortunately, his shop was adjacent to his brother's chemist shop and he obtained almost immediate relief by purchasing a box of *Fenniwragg's Patent Bile Tablets*.

Later, Thomas had the idea to organise battlefield tours to northern France, offering the chance to see at first hand the locations of major Great War battles. But he was ahead of his time and the tours ceased in 1917 after a number of holidaymakers were mortally wounded.

The company prospered in the 1930s when other travel firms were finding it hard, largely through Thomas' foresight in arranging holidays to Spain, where the Civil War was raging and prices were cheap.[1,2,3]

Footnotes

JMW BLUNT

1. Blunt began his career painting summer seascapes at Formby beach but he found the incessant rain, wind and cold temperatures unendurable.

GEORGE BERNARD BLUNT

1. Blunt's most successful work, *Pigmammalian*, ran for a season at the Oldham Coliseum but received mostly unfavourable reviews. The *Oldham Chronicle* described it as 'turgid stuff' and urged readers to avoid it like a dose of swine disease. *Pig Farmer Weekly* gave it five stars.

2. Uncle Bill's Meat-Free Meatballs were re-launched by Blunt Foods early in 2012.

THOMAS BLUNT

1. It was on a Thomas Blunt holiday to Spain that George Irwell wrote his celebrated work, *Homage to Catatonia*.

2. The company even attempted to revive interest in the gateaux tasting holidays to the Black Forest which had proven so popular in William Gladstone Blunt's day but without any great success. Public taste had moved on to Viennese Whirls and Thomas Blunt lost a lot of money on its German ventures.

3. Thomas Blunt & Son now operates exclusively as an internet travel agency.

Blunt's Tours poster c1913 (left). A nurse tends to the wounded as they return from one of Thomas Blunt's Battlefield Tours, c1916 (right).

Controversial adverts from Spaatchcock and Spaatchcock helped promote Uncle Joe's Rice Balls across Lancashire in 1932

JOHN BOYNTON BLUNT

John Boynton Blunt was the tenth child of William and Ernestina and was the only child born outside Wigan.

Ernestina was touring with Horace Miliband and His Performing Frogs in 1894 and had just stepped off stage during a matinee performance at the Bradford Alhambra when she went into labour. She gave birth to John at St Luke's Hospital before returning to the stage for the evening show.[1]

After leaving school, John started work as a junior clerk in a cotton mill not far from his father's Mortimer Street factory.

He took a night class in creative tattooing at St Martins College but soon realised he wasn't cut out for skin art and began writing articles for local papers such as *The Wigan Chronicle and Echo* and *The Parbold Standard*.

JB Blunt also wrote a series of novels which publishers rejected almost as fast as he produced them. Undeterred, he moved on to write dramas and had some minor success with one play in particular. *A Sanitary Inspector Calls* was based on a visit to a local fish and chip shop by council inspector Ralph Biggins and became a popular production with Wigan repertory companies in the 1930s.

In 1954, it was made into a film by 20th Century Spatchcock starring Alastair Simples and George Coalman (a later favourite of Spatchcock) in one of his first bit-parts.

WD & HO BLUNT

Henry Osset Blunt was the 12th child of William and Ernestina Blunt.

At school, Henry could often be found behind the bike shed selling his father's thin cheroots to his classmates for profit. It was no great surprise, therefore, that his careers teacher advised him to consider purchasing his own tobacconists. He was fortunate when one came on the market in Mintball Square after the Great War.

He persuaded his cousin William David to partner him and they opened their shop in December 1918. Henry was a kindly fellow and when the half-deaf sign writer he engaged to paint their shop frontage made a mistake, he hadn't the heart to tell him to correct it. Instead, Henry sourced a supply of toboggans which he retailed at the back of the shop, much to William's annoyance.

They managed to sell one or two, mainly in December and January, but for the rest of the year the toboggans stood gathering dust at the back of the shop. In 1920, tragedy struck when Henry was killed during an unfortunate tobogganing accident – three toboggans stacked on a shelf fell on him.

WD Blunt retired from the shop to develop industrial lubricant.[1] Henry's widow, Woodbine, (pictured above) continued to run the store for a number of years but it was an uphill struggle. She was forced to close in 1928 when, following several very mild winters, everything went downhill.

AJP BLUNT

Albert Jedward Pokemon Blunt was the self-appointed historian of the Blunt family. His forthright and excoriating historical commentary did not always make him popular with other members of the family.

Born in 1906, he was the youngest child of William Gladstone and Ernestina Blunt. He studied applied engineering at Wigan College of Mechanical Engineering and Applied Mining before discovering an interest in social history while observing local men and women celebrating Bluntsday. Like many of his contemporaries, AJP Blunt subsequently went to Oxford, spending almost half an hour there during a comfort break on a coach holiday to Devon.

Blunt was a prolific writer and published at least a dozen books a year. Although almost all are now out of print, they are worth tracking down and occasionally show up in bargain bookshops. AJP Blunt was for many years engaged in a bitter academic feud with Marxist historian Eric Hobnob, which culminated in Blunt punching Hobnob during a live interview with Frank Boffin on *Wake Up, Britain!* in 1985. Blunt sustained some minor abrasions but was subsequently offered his own history programme on late night BBC 2, much to Hobnob's disgust.

AJP Blunt lived in semi-retirement in a bungalow outside Bickershaw until his death in 2012.

AJP BLUNT'S PUBLICATIONS

Most of Blunt's books are currently out of print but his most notable publications are:

The Secret History of Wilhelm Stumpf und Söhne GmbH (1972) draws heavily on a series of letters discovered by *Sunday Times* journalists and authenticated by Blunt and a number of other noted scholars. Wilhelm Stumpf und Söhne attempted to suppress the book, arguing there was no basis in fact for the suggestion that the firm had bankrolled the Nazi party between the wars.

Emmanuel (1974) is the unofficial biography of Emmanuel Shiverofski, the so-called unsung hero of fridge magnet history. Blunt challenges the view that Shiverofski was 'conveniently airbrushed from the history books' by William Gladstone Blunt by concentrating on source material in the Blunt family archives, including a hitherto unpublished letter from Queen Victoria thanking WG Blunt for his kindness in sending her a fridge magnet, but questioning its purpose. Scientific analysis later revealed that the letter had almost certainly been written on a piece of Basildon Bond notepaper purchased from a newsagents sometime in 1973. Nevertheless, *Emmanuel* remains AJP Blunt's best-selling work.

The Man Who Is Half Man And Half Biscuit— Fact or Fiction? (1979) debunks the received wisdom that The Morocconi Brothers' notorious freak show exhibit, The Man Who Is Half Man And Half Biscuit, actually existed. Using source material from the Peak Frean Assortment Archive, Blunt demonstrates that Ennio Morocconi had enough skill to produce a man-sized biscuit which would fool thousands of visitors to the show.

Footnotes

JOHN BOYNTON BLUNT
1. John Boynton was not the only Blunt child to be born whilst Ernestina was working. She famously interrupted a performance at Wigan's Court Theatre in 1897 with the line 'I'm just nipping off for a cigarette' before returning to the stage half an hour later having been safely delivered of John Henry Blunt.

WD & HO BLUNT
1. Unable to think of a suitable name, he considered combining his initials with his wife's age and planned to call the product WD39. She insisted it be renamed WD21.

APPENDIX

When I told my publisher that it was my intention to include references to Stockport and Birkenhead in this book, he blanched a little and insisted on adding the subtitle *and Parts Of Cheshire and the Wirral*. Although I wasn't keen, I reluctantly agreed so as not to offend the residents of those two fine areas.

Strictly speaking, however, this should not have been necessary. As any local historian worth his (Cheshire) salt knows, Stockport and Birkenhead were once part of the historic county of Lancashire which stretched from the Irish Sea in the west to the North Sea in the east; Cheshire in the south and Durham in the north. Even today, there are those who claim that the Cheshire is part of Lancashire and Wirral is part of Cheshire.

In fact, at one time Lancashire made up almost half the area of England and had ambitions to take over Durham and Northumberland and parts of Wales.[1]

Few people know that Lancashire once actually extended several miles into the Irish Sea, but towns such as Seapool St Mark's, Widdrington and Warness have been lost to the waves.

The historic boundary of Lancashire almost exactly matches the area where tripe consumption was at its highest; even today, it is rarely eaten outside of the ancient boundary areas.

Their populations dwindled as they became engulfed by the waves and only the strongest swimmers and those who were expert at treading water were able to survive. Today, there are fewer than a dozen inhabitants of these submerged towns remaining, eking a meagre existence from fishing and scuba diving holidays.

The county boundary has fluctuated throughout history, particularly and most dramatically during the Wars of the Roses when the residents of Leeds or Manchester could find themselves living in Yorkshire one week and Lancashire the next.[2] This has continued down the years due to local government re-organisation. In 1891, the border town of Todmorden had to be moved

Lancashire during the Wars of The Roses (July 1480)

Lancashire during the Wars of the Roses (July 1481)

50 yards east whilst Barnoldswick moved in the opposite direction as part of the same arrangement. The residents of Barnoldswick refused to budge and existed as an enclave of Yorkshire inside Lancashire until they were forced to surrender after just two weeks when they were cut off by the Lancashire Electricity Board.

More recently, in 1962, Saddleworth became part of Lancashire but the cost of moving the small Pennine villages of Diggle and Dobcross brick by brick and the inconvenience caused was such that subsequent changes have involved moving the boundary rather than the buildings themselves.

The boundary with Cheshire is less controversial and has remained more or less the same for more than 1,000 years. Historically, it marks the line beyond which lived the Poshae, a tribe whose men drove expensive four wheeled chariots. Their women dyed their hair blonde and their bodies orange and wore garments made of fur but no undergarments. Today the boundary separates those who earn less than the national average wage from those who earn at least double. The population of Cheshire has been swelled by the southward migration of wealthy Lancastrians in search of cleaner air and cheaper salt.[3]

Lancashire's boundary fluctuations can be traced in maps, the most notorious of which is the so-called Filthie Mappe, purportedly drawn up in 1610 by the dyslexic cartographer, John Seed.

The map caused such offence that Seed was hung, drawn and quartered. It was only later discovered that the map had been drawn up by a trainee on a work experience programme whilst Seed was signed off work with the plague.

John Seed's so-called Filthie Mappe (1610) which led to his premature death

The Lancashire Hundreds c. 1250

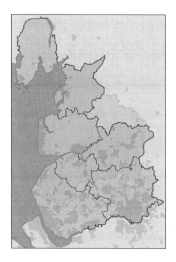

The Lancashire Thousands c. 1250

The county was originally divided into one hundred hundreds. As the county boundaries were subsequently redrawn, only six hundreds remained: Amounderness, Blackburn, Leyland, Lonsdale, Salford and West Derby. Planning permission for a further four hundreds was denied. The system was an early teaching tool intended to help children to count. Each hundred consisted of ten tens, with ten hundreds making a thousand. This was abolished when imperial weights and measures were introduced in the 14th century but has survived in the popular cupcake covering of 'hundreds and thousands'.

Footnotes

1. In Roman times, Lancashire was part of Northumbria which, as the name suggests, the Romans considered to be the northernmost district of the province of Umbria. The major towns of Northumbria were Durham, Gateshead and Assisi and its most important products were coal and olive oil.

2. The Wars Of The Roses were originally fought by the red rose of Lancaster, the white rose of York and the yellow rose of Texas. The Texans were forced to withdraw after the first battle for logistical reasons.

3. Lancashire and Cheshire were once separated by Adrian's Wall, a defensive fortification built by Adrian Fortescue-Smythe, a leader of the Poshae, to keep out marauding tribes from the north. It was destroyed by the Mancae in 652AD.

SELECT BIBLIOGRAPHY*

Myths and Legends of Lancashire and Parts of Cheshire — Graham Spatchcock

Biscuit Production in Interwar Lancashire: A Marxist Analysis — Professor Eric Hobnob

A Brief History of The Failsworth Pole Dancing Club — G Stringfellow

A Brief History of Meatballs — Professor Stephen Hawkeye

Let's Talk Tripe — Stuart Balls

A Brief History of Briefs — Selwyn Marks and Cyril Spencer

A Brief History of Brief Histories — Tristram Blunt

The Lost Tribes of Lancashire — Dr D J Ripley

Sir Alan Blunt's Book of How to Do Business — Sir Alan Blunt

Uncle Bill's Book of Lancashire Italian Recipes — W M Blunt

Charles and Maurice Spaatchcock's Big Book of Adverts — C & M Spaatchcock

Hankie Goes to Hollinwood — Rev. Charles Hankie

A Brief History of Biscuits — Nigella Huntley and Kirsty Palmer

A History of The World in 100 Fridge Magnets — Ian MacGregor

The Book of Nineteenth Century Look-Alikes — AJP Blunt

Practical Surveying for Toddlers — William Teflon

The Ladybird Book of Civil Engineering

The Civil Engineering Book of Ladybirds

The Ladybird Book of Ladyboys

The Book of Sharp Practices — Cecil Sharp

The Complete Lord Timothy Parker Stories — W W Blunt

My First Big Book of Maps — Anon.

A Brief History of Train Timetables — George Dent

The Condition of the Middle Class in England — Charles Marcus and Frederick Spangles

The Capitalist Manifesto — Charles Marcus and Frederick Spangles

The Theory of Buy One Get One Free — Charles Marcus and Frederick Spangles

The Collected Poems of Henry Cooper-Clarke edited by Melvyn Blunt

Hollinwood Babylon — Kenneth Banger

* All books are currently out of print unless otherwise indicated

OTHER BOOKS BY TMB

Coming Soon:

Stranger Than Fact: Mysteries of Lancashire

Forgotten Yorkshire

Tripe: A Social History

The Lost Films of 20th Century Spatchcock

The Visitor's Guide to Lancashire

Coming Soon from TMB Books
The Visitor's Guide to Lancashire
by
Dr Derek J Ripley

Lancashire's got the lot — sea, mountains, historic towns and tripe. So why spend a fortune on an expensive overseas holiday when you can spend a fortune on a holiday at home? Plus you won't have to waste money on sun cream. The TMB Visitor's Guide to Lancashire takes you to places other guide books don't and shows you the real Lancashire behind the tourist information centre blurb.

FLEETWOOD

The town of Fleetwood is famous for many things. Fleetwood's latest claim to fame is that it is the home of the Football League's newest football club — Fleetwood Town. It is also renowned as the birthplace of Lady Gaga and the home of one of the Seven Wonders of Lancashire — the Pharos. But there's more to Fleetwood than Fleetwood Town, Lady Gaga and the Pharos.

Most of all it is famous for fish. Fleetwood enjoys a most temperate micro-climate. The temperature rarely falls below freezing in the winter and rarely exceeds freezing in the summer. This climate is perfect for fish to multiply in the grey coastal waters.

A walk round this sleepy fishing village reveals its love affair with all things Piscean. Fleetwood Sea World is Fleetwood's celebration of the world of the sea. It is a completely natural visitor experience with no buildings and no tourist traps. It simply consists of beach and sea. Watch the tide come in then watch it go out, completely free of charge.

In the centre of the town there is a memorial to the cod wars of the 1970s in which millions of cod lost their lives. This is commemorated on 6th June every year when the residents of Fleetwood wear their trousers at half mast.

Fleetwood is the birthplace of the Fleetwood mac, a raincoat which protects the Fleetwood fisherman from the worst excesses of the Fleetwood weather and the Fleetwood windbreaker, a type of cagoule which protects other fishermen from the flatulence caused by excessive consumption of raw fish.

And, of course, Fleetwood is the home of one of the nation's favourite sweets — Pescatorean Pals, a delicious confection designed to warm the cockles of the Fleetwood fisherman's heart on the coldest winter's day. The recipe is secret but is reputed to contain jalapeno chilli powder, Vindaloo curry powder and cayenne pepper.

Famous Fleetwoodians include the UK's first all male dance troupe Cockles and Muscles, Mick Fleetwood, Margaret Thatcher, Sandie Shaw, Prince Harry, Simon Cowell, Beyoncé , Paris Hilton and Lady Gaga.

Top ten things to do in Fleetwood
1. Watch Fleetwood Town
2. Visit the Pharos
3. Visit Sea World
4. Visit the birthplace of Lady Gaga
5. Go fishing
6. Eat some fish and chips
7. Take a tram ride to Blackpool
8. Take a tram ride back to Fleetwood
9. Visit the University of Fleetwood
10. Watch TV

Coming Soon from TMB Books

Stranger Than Fact: Mysteries of Lancashire
by
Graham Spatchcock

Graham Spatchcock looks at the unexplained phenomena which make Lancashire the most mysterious county in the north west of England, apart from Cheshire and parts of the Wirral.

There are an unusually large number of ghost sightings in Lancashire. According to census data, in 1881 there were over 2,000 ghosts resident in Lancashire.

Spatchcock believes that this is because Lancashire was once part of the continent of America and lies on an old Red Indian burial ground. Movements of the earth's tectonic plates separated the continents more than 400 years ago.

He makes a convincing case for locating the legendary kingdom of Camelot near Charnock Richard. He believes the Camelot theme park is built on the site of the legendary Camelot as its proximity to the M6 would have enabled King Arthur to mobilise his knights at short notice and cites as further evidence the existence of the Chorley Round Table just a few miles away.

Spatchcock explores the mysterious Weavers' Triangle, an area astride the Leeds — Liverpool canal that was once at the heart of Burnley's textile industry and asks why narrow boats keep disappearing there.

The book includes a guide to the Seven Wonders of Lancashire - the Pharos of Fleetwood, the Tower of Blackpool, the Great Pyramid of Stockport, the Hanging Baskets of Tottington, the Coliseum Ballroom Of Rhodes and the Taj Mahal restaurant, Leyland.

He also investigates the mysteries surrounding the Great Pyramid which, he believes, is much more than just a call centre for the Co-operative Bank. Why did the architect choose the pyramid shape? Is there a secret chamber inside the Pyramid? What is buried beneath it? And why are so many mysterious flashing lights seen over the Pyramid at night (apart from its proximity to Manchester Airport)?

ABOUT THE AUTHOR

Derek J Ripley has an unrivalled passion for local history which dates back longer than he can remember. Born in Preston but brought up in Manchester and Wigan, he has lived at various times in Barrow-in-Furness, Blackpool, Kendal, Chester and Bury. He was educated in Bolton and Lancaster. His job as a local government librarian has seen him working in Southport, Ormskirk, Liverpool, Warrington, Knutsford, Altrincham, Stockport and Wilmslow. He now lives in Birkenhead and commutes daily to his job in Morecambe which sadly leaves him little time to pursue his favourite pastimes.

Derek has published widely on local history matters, earning him the soubriquet *'Mister History'* in his local pub, where he is vice-captain of the quiz team. When he is not reading about or writing local history, Derek likes to unwind with a game of bowls and in 2002, came third in the North West Lancashire Crown Green Bowls Championships. A keen cyclist and camper, Derek is a lover of the great outdoors and has an ambition to write a series of travel guides to some of the places sometimes overlooked by traditional tourist books. Derek is passionate about books. His favourite novelist is Patricia Highsmith and his favourite film is *The Talented Mr. Ripley.*

Derek professes to be a great fan of Waterstones and WH Smith bookshops as well as local independent book retailers — particularly when they champion local history and have a good café. Derek likes nothing better than sitting down in a bookshop with a nice café latte and a couple of good history books.

He is an avid listener — and sometime contributor to — local radio.

Derek is married to Nataya whom he met at a local history convention in Bangkok in 2008 and is currently working on his next project, *The Lost Films of 20th Century Spatchcock,* due for publication in October 2012.

He is a keen follower of Leeds United.

T M B
BOOKS

Bringing tripe to the bookshops of Britain since 2012

ISBN:
978 0 9573141 1 5

£9.99

THE LOST FILMS OF 20th CENTURY SPATCHCOCK

"Worth saving up £9.99 for"
Martin Sixsmith

"At last—the definitive appreciation of Spatchcock!
Anyone who has managed to get through From Here To
Maternity or Wendy Does Wigan will want - and need -
this book."
Andy Kershaw

"Hilarious!"
Billy Butler, BBC Radio Merseyside

"Not my cup of tea"
SG Holt, Radcilffe Mercury

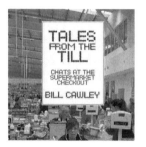

ISBN:
978 0 9573141 3 9
£4.99

TALES FROM THE TILL

Over 300 snippets of conversation and observation from
the other side of the checkout.

A one man Mass Observation survey that shines a
spotlight on contemporary shopping.

Wry, witty and sometimes moving!

Available at all good bookshops, Amazon.co.uk and via
www.tripemarketingboard.co.uk/books

Coming soon from TMB Books

Based on research undertaken by the Tripe Marketing
Board's official historian Dr Derek J Ripley for the
inauguration of World Tripe Day, this remarkable book
looks at the part tripe has played in the history of Britain
and the World since the dawn of mankind.

How did man first decide that the stomach of a cow was
palatable—and why?

Dr Ripley's book aims to answer these and other
questions that have tantalised and intrigued scholars
and tripe lovers for centuries.

Printed in Great Britain
by Amazon